The Red Foil

an SF Mystery

by t.santitoro

The Red Foil
By t.santitoro

Story copyright owned by t.santitoro
Cover illustration by t.santitoro
Cover design by Marcia A. Borell

First Printing, August 2024

Hiraeth Publishing
P.O. Box 1248
Tularosa, NM 88352
e-mail: hiraethsubs@yahoo.com

Also by t.santitoro

Adopted Child

The Legend of Trey Valentine

The Saint & The Demon (with Ron Sparks)

Those Who Die

To the Gilded Quills—you know who you are. Thanks to all of you for your continued encouragement and support!

ONE

When I let myself into Tayla Block's quarters aboard the space mining station, two things hit me at once: the chill air, and the pungent aroma. She'd been cooking her 'hodge-podge' again, and the smell of exotic spices permeated the recycled air, despite the station's filters.

I wrinkled my nose, and moved further into her quarters, searching. She was still on duty, and this was a rare opportunity to retrieve some of my things. There were only two rooms to check: a living area and a hygienic chamber.

Her living room, as usual, was a tumbled mess of colorful pillows and throws, as her quarters were located far from the main generators, and were always cooler than she preferred, as evidenced by the present temperature. Both the bed and the g-couch were rumpled and covered with clothing and various odds and ends. I scanned the space quickly, picking up one of my rec-sets that I found tangled in a throw on the couch. The pink one, the one Tayla had liked to borrow all the time. I stood motionless for a moment, feeling the cool, pink rec-set wires in my hand, then continued my search. I found an oversized sweatshirt that was mine--one that Tayla had always worn to bed--and a photo of us that was taken on Olympus Mons two stan'ars ago. I paused, staring at our happy images, as memories of our holiday and Tayla's laughter briefly halted my progress.

The sound of dripping broke into my reverie, and dragged my attention to the galley. The small, stainless steel section on the far side of the room was illuminated by a malfunctioning light--the one she always left on when she went out--and the short, brushed-steel surface of the counter was strewn with dirty utensils and dishes, as though she'd started cleaning up after her meal, but had been interrupted. Water dripped from the sink faucet, and I tightened the handle without thinking, an old habit.

A box of cookies sat askew on the built-in table. Sweets were a luxury, an expensive commodity in space. Curious, I glanced at the label.

Huh! They were imported. From the outer quadrant, no less. I took one, and bit in, appreciating the high-quality flavor. She must have gotten a massive raise, to be able to afford something this expensive.

Still chewing, I started to turn away, when something caught my eye. A tiny bit of gift wrap still clung to the corner of the cookie box, its red foil reflecting the flickering light.

I hesitated, my throat constricting, and I found it hard to swallow the sample cookie.

So. She had moved on already? The cookies were a *gift?*

My breath caught in a sob, and I forced the cookie down, fighting a sudden urge to break into tears. What was the use in crying? Apparently Tayla had moved on.

In an effort to battle the panic that was rising in my chest, I methodically checked the confines of the HC. Nothing else of mine remained in Tayla's quarters. I shakily gathered the few items that I'd found, glanced once more around the area that we used to share and, placing her extra access card on a table, let myself out.

***

I didn't sleep well that night.

I'd put on the oversized sweat shirt I'd retrieved, and cried myself to sleep, only to wake constantly from dreams of Tayla, my pillow damp.

When she'd asked me to move out, I hadn't thought that there was anyone else involved, as we were seriously fond of each other. But Tayla and I weren't exactly compatible, as far as being roomies. She was a bit of a slob, and I suffered from OCD, so I suppose our parting was probably inevitable. After almost three full stan'ars of shared accommodations, several nasty arguments over the state of her quarters had convinced us both that we were better off living apart, and I'd returned to my own abandoned quarters on a different deck. We'd parted on friendly terms, though, and were continuing to see each other, as our schedules aboard the space station allowed.

That she had been seeing someone else stunned me. My mind's eye kept returning to that speck of red foil gift wrap on the box of cookies, wondering. Who aboard the mining station could afford to give that kind of gift?

Although it was still early, I dragged myself out of bed, and went over the duty roster in my mind, as I crossed the room to use the HC, but none of the people on the list had the means to import gifts from the outer quadrant. So, who?

In the narrow confines of the HC, I stared at my image in the stainless mirror above the shallow, metal sink. I looked like shit. No wonder Tayla had been seeing someone else. Five stan'ars on the space station had worn lines into the corners of my grey eyes, and around my mouth. I searched my features, and saw what changes constant worry had made, and knew that I looked older than my 27 stan'ars. And now, added to that, my eyes were red rimmed and bloodshot, my nose pink. I turned away from the evidence of my emotions, and blew my nose, still thinking.

Who was Tayla seeing?

I used the toilet, flushing twice because the plumbing on this deck wasn't the best, and left the HC, pulling the sweatshirt off over my head as I went. For once, I dressed without even seeing the clothes that I was donning.

I popped a FreezieKelp cake into the nuker, but the sweet smell of it only resulted in turning my stomach, and I threw it into the recycle, wiping angrily at a tear that had escaped and run down my cheek.

Tayla! WHY?

I wandered back into the HC, brushed my teeth and ran a hand through my close-cropped copper hair; put on some lip stain. I stared at myself in the mirror, determined to be strong.

"Just ASK her!" I told myself, sharply. Tayla was used to my directness. She was due to come off her shift any time, and I could catch her on her way to her quarters, and talk to her.

Little did I know, that I'd never get the chance.

***

I didn't catch Tayla after all. But it was still too soon for me to go on duty and, rather than go back to my solitary quarters and brood, I found myself entering the Perihelion Cafe.

Even at this early hour, the Perihelion was crowded with a mixture of people just going off-duty, and those waiting around to begin their shifts. The cafe was a quirky place, all color and noise and motion, a corner of the station that was at once Boho and noir, topped with the all-pervasive scent of brewing coffee.

At my entrance, several long-timers glanced in my direction, and a sudden hush fell over the cafe. I gave my order at the counter, picked up my coffee, and proceeded into the dining area. I saw a few of my co-workers and their friends, seated in a booth in the far back, and started in their direction, mindful of the awkward silence that had descended over the place.

The smell of strong coffee and sweet kelp cakes wafted over me as I went, leaving a heavenly aroma in my wake, but I was too self-conscious to be aware of it. As I reached the back of the cafe, quiet conversation resumed around me, and I plopped into the round booth, giving everybody a puzzled look.

"'Sup?" I asked nonchalantly, throwing a glance behind me, to indicate the odd behavior of the other patrons. I took a delightful sip of my latte, then swallowed, waiting for a reply.

"Haven't you heard?" demanded a petite, blond girl sitting across from me in the booth. She was the friend of another rocket-horse jockey, and I struggled for her name.

"Heard? Heard what?" I hadn't exactly been open to gossip lately, so withdrawn had I been over the fact of Tayla's new love interest. I took another drink of the steamy, delicious warmth, savoring its flavor.

10

The blond, whose name I suddenly remembered was Millie Something-or-Other, shifted her glance from me, to the others at our table, and back.

"Tayla Block's gone missing." She replied in a small voice. "She didn't report for her shift, and no one's seen her."

I almost spit out the coffee I'd just sipped, but I choked it down.

"What?" I asked hoarsely.

I'd heard the words, but they hadn't made any sense. How could one "go missing" aboard a space station? It wasn't as if you could take a long walk off a short pier, or anything. She would have had to sign out a rocket-horse, or something, if she'd gone off station, and she wasn't even certified to fly one. She had to be *some*where.

Millie gave me a blank look, the kind of look that betrayed her emotional shock, and I all at once realized that she was seriously upset.

With that unwelcome realization, the coffee residue on my tongue suddenly tasted bitter.

Tayla Block, my lover and ex-roommate, had disappeared.

TWO

The interview was as unsettling as the news of Tayla's disappearance had been.

The station's Chief Security Investigator was a big man named Gai Hao. At first glance, Hao looked like someone's grandfather. His features, set in a fleshy frame of cheeks and chins, seemed rather soft and kind. A second look told me that this gentleman was neither grandfatherly, nor kind. His lips were a tight slit, and his almond eyes held the brittle look of a viper about to strike.

We were in the security office, a place that was both sterile and cold, lacking furniture beyond the chief's desk and chair, which faced a hard bench built into the adjacent wall. White LED lights blazed down from the ceiling, giving the small room a stark appearance.

I was perched on the bench, my arms covered in goose bumps, my jaws clenched to avoid the chattering which would betray my discomfort--and my dismay. Hao's bulk loomed behind the cluttered desk. He leaned forward, expectantly.

I responded to the question he'd put forth.

"Yeah, we're seeing each other--*were*--, "I corrected myself, feeling nonplussed. Whatever had happened to Tayla, it was safe to assume that we were no longer an "item", right? Again, that piece of red foil wrapping insinuated itself on my thoughts.

I should have been at work by now. My shift had started at least half an hour ago, yet here I was, being "interviewed" by this mountain of a man, and getting the distinct impression that he had me under suspicion. *Me!*

He said, "You are aware, are you not, that your fingerprints were found all over Ms. Block's quarters?"

Of course they were! I'd lived there, for the better part of three stan'ars! But, instead of provoking Hao with my sarcasm, I said quietly, "Yes, until recently, we were lovers."

"Until recently? Until *how* recently?"

I cleared my throat. "She asked me to leave a--uh--few weeks ago." My words died off, lame. I knew how this sounded, what the investigator must be thinking.

He didn't disappoint me. "Asked you to leave? How forcibly did she ask?"

My face colored. "We quarreled--"

The Chief of Security nodded. "Did this argument get violent?"

"--*NO!*" I stood up, shouting.

"Siddown!" he ordered. I sat. "Just where *is* Tayla Block?"

"I don't know," I said, wearily. "I didn't even know she was missing, until co-workers told me." I looked up. "Am I--being detained?"

"No," growled the investigator. He stood and glared down at me. "But I'm freezing your mining and travel options."

I was aghast. "But, I haven't done anything! I need to run my rocket-horse for work--!"

"According to all reports, you were the last person to see Tayla Block alive. Need I say more? You're to stay put on this station until further notice, or unless Ms. Block is found."

I nodded miserably and got out of there as quickly as I could, not sure of exactly how much trouble I was in.

***

"I've been ordered confined to the station." I threw the keys to my rocket horse onto the HR manager's desk, as per Company regulations.

The HR office was located on the outer ring of the station, its exterior hull boasting a large view port from which one could gaze out at the field of asteroids we were mining. Beside the station, Rareterra Five, the largest of those asteroids--in actuality a small planetoid--turned in a stately counter rotation on the black backdrop of space. Also known as RTF, Rareterra Five was the company's main source of mining income, producing megatons of industrial minerals and gemstones annually.

At the neatly arranged 'lectro desk before the view port sat a youngish man, in his mid-to-late thirties, with perfectly styled dark hair and a suit that was precise in every detail. He had been studying his desk top vid-scope intently, unaware of my entrance, until I had announced my presence by tossing my keys onto his 'lectro desk.

Jimmer Graham glanced up in surprise at the sound of my keys hitting the shiny surface. He gave me a stern look of exasperation at the interruption.

"--and you *are*?" He ran his eyes over my features as if he'd never seen me before in his life, even though we'd met several times in the course of my career with the company.

"Soefee Sparrow. I run a rocket-horse above Rareterra Five--"

"Why aren't you at work?--I need every available rocket-horse working RTF's sector!" He growled. "What's this about, anyway?"

In the station's corridor outside the office, the clamor of employees on their way to their duties had died out as starting time had approached and passed. In the ensuing quiet, my mind raced.

So. The rumors about Tayla's disappearance hadn't reached the HR office? I gulped. I would have to confess my involvement in the Tayla Block situation, despite the fact that I really didn't think it was any of corporate's business. Tayla had vanished, *that* was their business, but our relationship had been personal, and I hated to divulge even the least part of it.

"Tayla Block has disappeared from the station. No one knows where she is."

The look in the HR manager's eyes changed subtly. He said, "Our chief geologist has gone missing? Why wasn't *I* notified?" As human resources manager on the station--as well as the asteroid belt that was being mined--he was in charge of all Company personnel.

I shrugged, raising my eyebrows as I did so, and he continued, "Anyway, what has this got to do with *you*?" He glanced briefly at the chronometer built into his desk, then back up at me, repeating his previous question. "It's past 05:00, why aren't you already on the job?"

"The Chief Security Investigator locked out my mining and travel options." I complained. "I--uh--was the last one to see Tayla before--before she--"

He stood, impatient, and cut off what I had been about to say, already ahead of me. "Have you been accused of anything?"

"N--no--" I began again, but again he interrupted.

"Then get to work. I'll handle Hao." And he turned abruptly away, to study RTF's slow rotation beyond his office view port, dismissing me without further consideration.

I studied his unyielding back for a moment, his figure silhouetted against the softly lit pink terrain of the planetoid outside, then slid my keys back off his desk.

Graham spoke once more, his back still to me, his voice less than compassionate.

"Oh, and Sparrow? Your pay'll be docked for being late."

My fist closed tightly around the rocket horse keys, digging them into my palm, and I stomped out of his office without even feeling their painful bite.
***

Still feeling the cold sting of Graham's indifferent dismissal, and my mind still in upheaval over Tayla's disappearance, I headed over to the garage, where I suited up, thinking.

Jimmer Graham had said he'd handle Chief Security Investigator Gai Hao. He must have contacted the man immediately following our discussion because, by the time I'd reached the equipment garage at the other end of Space Mining Station ALT 556, my mining and travel options had been reinstated. I wondered briefly how that was possible. I was pretty certain that the CSI had top priority over HR. Maybe I was wrong.

I slid into my heavy EVA suit and helmet, preparing to join my co-workers outside. I activated my com unit, as I strode over to my usual parking space.

The garage's docking bay was deserted around me, everyone else already at work hauling loads from RTF over to the refinery barge, and I could hear the jockey's chatter over the G-frequencies from inside my EVA helmet. It was a typical start to a day of work mining the asteroid belt.

Ol' Betty's engine started immediately upon inserting my key and pressing her ignition button. She was an older model rocket-horse, one that still required keys instead of a retinal scan, but she was sturdy and reliable, and I preferred her to the newer models. She was bright yellow, with the standard black striping, and dented as hell, but to me she was beautiful, and I grinned despite my turbulent thoughts, as I mounted the vehicle, and tugged the safety belts into place.

Beneath me, Ol' Betty purred, the vibration of her idling engine as gentle and comforting as any rocket-horse I had ever ridden. I straddled the saddle, the seat belts hugging my suit-encased body firmly. Grasping the joystick in my right hand, I turned to check my clearances.

As I glanced behind me, something caught my helmeted vision. There, on the tail end of Ol' Betty, was a thin white flap of mylar, stuck beneath the edge of my saddle.

I reached around, and was just able to grab the scrap with my gloved hand. I held it in front of my visor, surprised to find that there were words running across the slick surface, and they were addressed to me.

In the harsh lights of the garage, I read the brief message.

"Soefee. Important discovery. Gone to RTF. Tayla."

THREE

My heart almost stopped at the words I'd just read. For a long moment, my head spun, and I couldn't seem to focus. I stared at the shiny white-plastic mylar print-out that Tayla had left on my rocket horse, and my throat constricted. Tayla!

Memory of her soft closeness and lopsided grin tugged at my emotions, and I had to squeeze my eyes shut to prevent tears from blurring my vision. Crying in a helmet in null gravity was something I'd been advised against, and I didn't want to test the warning. My breath in my ears sounded too shallow and quick, and my suit's heart rate monitor showed an elevated level. I had to calm down and think clearly.

Good God, was Tayla still alive and somewhere on RTF? How could she have left the station without anyone knowing? Was it even possible that Tayla was down on Rareterra Five right now, perhaps enjoying the adventure of opening a new vein of minerals, or possibly even celebrating the success of discovering something super valuable?

Then reality set in, and I reconsidered: If Tayla had gone to RTF by choice, why hadn't she just told me--or even one of her colleagues in the science department--that she was going? Why the cryptic mylar message? What had she supposedly discovered? On the other hand, if she'd been abducted, perhaps this was a ruse. I had to wonder if this was a trap of some kind, designed to lure me down to RTF to cement my already suspicious-looking situation in the eyes of the law. As far as anyone else knew, I was a prime suspect in Tayla's disappearance, and forbidden to leave the Station. Going down to RTF might make me look guilty of something.

Was the message in my hand really even from Tayla? It was, after all, only a print-out. Anyone with access to a printer and the garage could have made it and placed it on my rocket horse. My mind raced with the possibilities of who had access to both. In the anxiety that had overcome me, my ideas just looped around back to the beginning again, and I was getting nowhere in my musings.

I was so lost in my roiling thoughts that I sat motionless on Ol' Betty, forgetting my surroundings, until the rocket horse's vibration insinuated itself into my speculations. At once the G-frequency chatter in my helmet grabbed my attention again, returning me to reality. I heard someone mention my name, in connection with Tayla's disappearance, and I straightened in the saddle. It would seem my co-workers shared Hao's suspicions.

I examined the mylar one last time, then glanced at the chronometer on my EVA suit's sleeve. I had little time to wonder about my find or its implications. I was already late, and had to get busy with my job, or be docked the entire day's pay. I shoved the bit of mylar into a pocket on my suit and sealed the flap.

The way I saw it, I had no choice but to investigate the possibility that the message really was from Tayla. I had to know if she was okay. As soon as my shift was over, I would be required to sign Ol' Betty back into the garage. After that, I would have to find an alternate way off the station.

One way or another, I was now determined to go down to Rareterra Five.

***

When my shift at work was through, and I'd parked Ol' Betty back in her usual spot in the garage, I had run my operator's card through the sign-out, and had then headed for the space docks.

While I'd spent my shift hauling rocks to the refinery barge with Ol' Betty, I'd been searching my memory for any other way to get off the station, and I'd suddenly remembered Millie Baxter. It had been Millie who'd broken the news to me, of Tayla's disappearance, and it occurred to me that Millie worked in the waste removal admin office. Built-up trash from the station was usually carried down to RTF by shuttle, where it was off-loaded and buried in old mine shafts. The waste removal shuttle was piloted by remote control, meaning no one

18

would even know if I was aboard. There were no life support systems on the vessel, but I'd known that I would already been wearing my EVA suit, so it wasn't an issue. I'd gone down to the dock area, found the departing waste removal shuttle, and had easily secreted myself aboard.

So here I was now, just entering the *Smuggler's Den* tavern through its rock-composed tunnel airlock, where I finally doffed my EVA suit, hung it in a locker, and became reacquainted with one-g. Following a day of zipping about in zero-g on my rocket-horse, full gravity pulled at my body with its unwelcome weight, and I almost tripped exiting the airlock into the tavern's main room.

The *Smuggler's Den* on RTF was exactly what it sounded like: a hole-in-the-wall catch-all of the scurviest-looking smattering of humanity you could ever possibly imagine. But it was also the most popular bar in the planetoid's only settlement, frequented by miners, buyers, smugglers and administrators alike and, as such, I knew it was the best place to start my search for Tayla.

The taproom was barely lit, with raw corundum walls that glittered here and there in the dimness. There was a stench to the place that could only be described as the stale odor of desperation. Miners perched atop metal stools at the bar, their worn faces relaxed into a semblance of numb emptiness, and in the corner, a round booth held a few sales execs and buyers in spotless suits. I headed for the bar.

The man tending bar looked to be in his late twenties, with a shaved head, deep dimples on either side of his mouth, and an upside-down triangle of short dark facial hair beneath his lower lip. The name tag on his apron said his name was Jicob. He was polishing the sleek surface of the counter with a white cloth, and gave me a smile as I stepped up.

"What'll you have?" he asked, the age-old question seeming oddly noir coming from him. He had a voice that was soft and deep, with a refined accent that seemed out-of-place for the paltry surroundings, but his grin was friendly enough.

"Information." I spoke as quietly as possible, to keep the conversation between just the two of us. Luckily there were no patrons seated nearby. I reached into my work overalls, and produced a small laminated photo of Tayla and me on vacation to Olympus Mons. "Do you recognize this woman? Has she been in here recently?" My questions had the panicked sound of impending despair, and I winced inwardly at my uncontrolled emotions.

Jicob studied the photo intently for a long moment. He looked up, and our eyes met. He had clear green eyes with little flecks of gold in them, and his gaze seemed to swallow me whole. I glanced quickly away, feeling myself blush, which was odd because I wasn't interested in men.

He said, "She's been in here before, but not in a long time."

I could feel my face fall in disappointment, but I forced myself to ask, "Alone?"

Jicob answered immediately. "No. She was always with someone. One of the big wigs."

One of the execs? I swallowed hard, knowing it would have taken a large pay rate to have afforded Tayla's box of cookies with the red foil gift wrap. Had Tayla been seeing one of the company's higher-ups, then? Or someone from the outside? A buyer, maybe?--which could possibly explain Tayla's imported luxury from the outer quadrant. I needed clarification.

I said, "An equipment sales rep? A buyer maybe?"

But Jicob shook his head, and continued wiping the bar, as if discussing the difference between brands of lagers. He seemed to recognize my need for discretion. He said quietly, "No. Much higher up. Home world admin, maybe. Somebody important." He reached down a bottle from the shelf behind him, and poured a scant amount into a shot glass, murmuring. "On the house."

I dipped my head in thanks, took the glass and threw back the shot. A warm sensation immediately flooded my throat and spread its way slowly into my stomach. I grinned despite myself.

"Would you recognize the person again?"

He said nothing, but nodded his bald head, then took down another bottle and again poured a shot. Handing it to me, our eyes met again. He said pointedly, "*Neither* of them has been in here recently."

I did the second shot, gave him a grateful nod, put the empty glass on the bar, and turned to go.

But Jicob stopped me with his next words. They were quietly uttered, almost mixing in with the conversations around us. "You forgot this." I spun around and he handed back the photograph of Tayla and me that he'd still been holding. He indicated the person standing with me at the base of the great Martian volcano.

Then, so softly that I could hardly make out what Jicob was saying, he spoke once more. "Don't know how true it is, but I--hear she's dead."

***

With Jicob's quiet statement, my legs almost went out from under me, and I had to grab onto the bar to keep my balance.

The barkeep saw my reaction, and came around the end of the counter, concern edging his voice.

"Are you alright?"

I nodded, my heart pounding in distress over the rumor that Tayla might actually be dead.

Referring to my physical response, he said, "Were the shots too much?"

I'd drunken myself into a stupor several times in my life, and never had it been a short journey, so the question provoked a sharp bark of laughter.

"No. It--it's just--" I glanced at the photo in my hand, and my eyes blurred.

The bartender said, "I'm sorry. You were--close?"

I nodded and gulped back an urge to spill my entire history with Tayla all over his easy-listener persona. Instead, I found myself asking, "Where did you hear that--that--that she's--?"

"Hey! How 'bout s'm service over here?" demanded a customer farther down the bar.

Jicob gave me an apologetic look, and went back behind the counter, to tend to his patron. I stood for a moment, collecting myself and watching him return to his work, then put the photo back into the pocket of my overalls, and left the *Smuggler's Den*.

***

Once again aboard the station, I slammed my hand down onto the chief security investigator's cluttered desk. This time it was me looming over him, the bright LEDs putting shadows on all three of his chins.

Rather than be intimidated by my action, Gai Hao squinted up at me with inscrutable calm. "--And how, exactly, did you get off the station and down to RTF?" he asked, in response to my apprising him of what I'd found out on the planetoid.

I straightened in the chill office, and turned away from his question. "That's none of your damn business. I want to know why nothing's being done! It's all over Rareterra Five that Tayla's--dead." I turned back to face the security man, trying to sound stern despite the quaver in my voice. "What are you doing to find out whether or not it's true?"

Hao studied me in the stark white light, pursing his thick, rubbery red lips. "There's no evidence to suggest any such thing, and if there were, I'd have you in the station's lock-up already!"

"*Me*?" I couldn't believe what I'd just heard. "I loved--*love*--Tayla! And I'm the only one who's been trying to find her! If you'd just do your effing job--"

Gai Hao stood. He was a head and a half taller than me, and he leaned his flabby bulk over the crammed desk, his fat face frowning barely an eyelash from mine, his garlic-and-ginger spiced breath buffeting my cheeks.

"At this point, *Ms.* Sparrow, *you* are my only suspect. If you don't want your mining and travel privileges restricted again, I suggest you go back to *your* job, and forget all about me and *my* job. How I conduct my investigation, is none of your concern. Besides, I'm the *station's* chief security investigator; I have no jurisdiction on RTF. If anything has happened to Ms. Block on Rareterra Five, it's entirely out of my hands!"

22

I drew in a deep lung-full of his odorous exhalation, refusing to blink; not backing down. Inwardly, my guts quaked. I hadn't realized that Hao had no authority on RTF. Who was going to help me find out where Tayla was, and if she remained alive? Still a lash's length away from his glowering countenance, I summoned up all my bravado, and said through clenched teeth, "Don't threaten me, Hao. Just stay out of my way."

Then I spun around--

--And fled the scene.

***

I'm not one for confrontation, and my hands were still shaking by the time I got to my quarters; my anxiety almost at stroke-level. The fact that I had dared to threaten Hao left me more stunned than the argument itself.

I slipped my access card through the lock and escaped into my room, the lights automatically winking on, brightening the area with the warm glow of an early afternoon sun. Everything was exactly as I'd left it, and I heaved a deep sigh, relief flooding over me. Crossing the area, I kicked off my scuffs, and dropped onto the bed, emotionally spent.

After my few hours spent on RTF, I had little hope that Tayla was still alive. Once I'd left the *Smuggler's Den*, I'd visited the settlement's other two taverns, only to have Jicob's tale repeated almost verbatim: Tayla had been seen on RTF several times, always in the company of an admin official, but neither had been seen in awhile. I'd tried prying information out of the receptionist at the stay-awhile, but the roboid hadn't responded to my queries with much more than one-word answers. So much for 'customer service' programming. I'd spent almost four hours on RTF, only to become more confused than ever.

It was looking more likely that the rumors were true, and the fact that Gai Hao wouldn't--or couldn't--do anything about the situation frightened me. Upon my return to the station, I'd asked around the *Perihelion Cafe*, but no one would give me the time of day, let alone any answers concerning Tayla. What had happened to Tayla

23

Block, and why wasn't anything being done about finding her? Who was in charge of security on RTF, and how could I contact them, when I didn't even know who they were? If Tayla really was dead, who had left the mylar note on my rocket-horse, and for what reason? Why had everyone on the station suddenly become so tight-lipped about her disappearance?

The only real information I had to go on, was the fact that everyone on RTF had mentioned seeing Tayla several times in the company of some corporate higher-up. Who that person was, I had no idea. Wondering about it now, the idea niggled at me.

Had Tayla really been seeing someone else romantically?

My heart ached. I rolled over on the bed and something in my overalls poked me. I reached into my pocket and pulled out the laminated photo of me and Tayla. I gazed at her crooked smile and laughing eyes. My throat tightened and I hugged the picture to my heart. I lay that way for a long time, as the sounds of the great space station gently lulled me into a deep, dreamless sleep.

***

I sprang awake just moments before my alarm went off.

With a groan, I dragged myself out of bed, still wearing my rumpled overalls. I got into the shower. Washed, rinsed, dried. Grabbed another set of work clothes. Dressed. All with the mechanical precision of routine.

Skipping breakfast, unable to eat, my mind still focused on the possibility of my ex-lover having cheated on me, and then being killed, my thoughts wouldn't coalesce into anything substantial. There was the box of cookies with the red foil wrap, and the sightings of Tayla with someone on RTF, neither of which pointed to a definite conclusion. All my suppositions just kept circling back to that lack of real evidence.

Down at the garage, I pulled my helmet and EVA suit out of the locker, still puzzling over the mysteries confronting me. I suited up, then left the locker room, and went out into the docking area. As usual, I activated my com unit before I strode over to my parking space, and immediately the chatter of other jockeys filled my ears with the inane banter of co-workers just starting their shift.

I inserted my key, pushed the ignition button, and Ol' Betty roared to life. I drew the safety harness about myself, clicking it securely into place. I checked my clearances, and we glided out of the garage on low propulsion.

Out into the zero-g vacuum of space we went, the wide, black vista seeming to open around us to accept our passage. In my helmet I heard the supervisor now exchanging daily instructions with the other jockeys. As I approached the cluster of workers, my boss greeted my arrival on the scene, then gave me my list of tasks, his voice in my ears sounding stiff and cold over the g-frequencies. I read between the lines. Even Dansk must share the suspicions about me. I acknowledged his assignments with a curt "Copy that." and proceeded to gun my rocket horse toward a waiting chunk of pink ore.

And then, without any warning, Ol' Betty exploded beneath me.

FOUR

The blast was silent, but I saw the brilliant flash and felt the shock wave that threw both me and my saddle clear of the spreading wreckage, hurtling me toward the surface of RTF at a dangerous velocity. Rareterra Five had just enough of a weak gravity well to capture me, or I might have sped off into the void, unable to get back to the station. As it was, the yellow-and-black debris of Ol' Betty swirled in my vision, kaleidoscoping around and around, chasing itself in my helmet's field of view, as my momentum took me nearer to an impending impact on the planetoid below me. I was helpless and in shock, not sure what had just happened.

After a moment of dazed stupefaction, my mind began functioning clearly again, and I remembered that, built into the back of my saddle, was an emergency parachute. I wondered if RTF's thin methane-and-carbon-dioxide atmosphere would be sufficient to open and then buoy up the chute. I just needed enough air for breaking the speed at which I was traveling. I was counting on the planetoid's relatively low gravity to do the rest.

I patted around on the edge of the saddle, my gloved hands searching for the emergency ring that was attached to the ejection cord, and found it. My hands trembled, as I fingered the chute ejection mechanism, waiting, despite the almost irresistible urge, to deploy the chute. "Not yet," I whispered to myself, "Not yet. *Don't pull the cord!*" If I deployed the parachute prematurely, it could slow my fall too quickly and might even rip the lines. I counted sixty long slow seconds and then finally pulled the ring.

Even though I was used to moving in zero-g, sudden deceleration often made me queasy, and when the chute deployed, yanking me harshly upward, my stomach lurched, too, and I almost threw up in my helmet. I squeezed my eyes shut, blocking out the spinning vista of Rareterra Five that was now below me, and tried not to retch.

"It's ok," I whispered into my helmet, "it's ok, it's ok. Just breathe." I'd only practiced emergency chute deployment and landing once, back when I'd first applied for a job with the company, but that was long ago, and my skills were worse than rusty. My body was positioned in a downward alignment regarding RTF--and its swiftly approaching terrain--with the back of my seat and the parachute above me. There were only minutes before I would crash land, and I attempted to go over the proper procedure in my mind, trying not to hyperventilate in my anxious state.

So busy was I, in trying to recall the correct method of landing, that I was stunned by the unexpectedly violent impact as I hit the ground. An "oof!" of air escaped my lungs, as the rocket-horse saddle slammed onto RTF, and the safety harness dug severely into my shoulders and across my body, as the saddle and I bounced twice before coming to a sudden stop on the surface.

My first reaction was a shaky, "I made it! I'm down!"

My second reaction was one of shock, as both the realization of what had occurred, and the pain of my injuries, washed over me at once. I was *not* ok. My entire body felt like it'd been rolled around in one of the company's giant rock tumblers. I'd gashed my head on the com gear in my helmet, and little balls of blood clung weakly against my visor.

For a long moment, I lay upside down, still encased in the safety belts on the saddle, on the hard pink soil of the planetoid. The startled chatter of dismayed voices that had accompanied my accident was gone from my ears, replaced by the disheartening static of dead communications. Great. No communications meant no rescue. For all anyone knew, I'd been killed in the explosion.

I reached a hand up to disengage the safety harness, and slowly removed the belts from my quaking body, clinging to the last strap as the low gravity threatened to lift me away from the heavy saddle. Righting myself was a bit tricky, but I managed the maneuver as cautiously as possible. Then, annoyed at the constant static, I switched off my useless com unit.

That's when I finally heard the hiss of escaping air.

A leak in my EVA suit! I clawed frantically at the saddle's storage compartment beneath the seat with my gloved hands, trying to open the catch and, when I succeeded, rummaged around in the exposed drawer for a quick-patch. Moments later, the leak found and securely sealed, I breathed a shaky sigh of relief. A quick check of my suit's readouts told me what I didn't want to know. I had no idea where on RTF I was, where the solitary settlement was located in relation to my position, and the readouts had just confirmed my air supply at only half-full.

A grim grin parted my lips and caused me to wince painfully at the action. At least I had acknowledged my air supply as half-full, rather than half-empty. Things were definitely looking up.

***

Scouting Rareterra Five's skyline for any sign of lights, brought only disappointment. With no visible sign of Dover settlement on the horizon, I had no choice but to begin walking. I salvaged what I could easily carry from the drawer beneath the saddle's seat. One spare canister of emergency air, a lantern, the patch kit, and a bulb of water. It wasn't much, but then it wasn't a lot to lug along with me on what could turn out to be a long journey, either.

I grabbed the gear and threw it into the provided mesh bag, and straightened, suddenly nauseous and dizzy. Wonderful. Nothing like a concussion to make a trek into the unknown even more memorable. I swung the bag over my shoulder and started out in the direction I hoped would lead me to Dover, my faltering steps more like hops and bobs in the low gravity, the beam of my lantern shining before me.

Jouncing carefully along the pink terrain, each strike of my feet on the uneven gravel adding to the pounding in my head, and hoping I would have enough oxygen to sustain me on my hike, I reflected on what had happened to Ol' Betty. No alerts had shown up on her dash to indicate that there was anything wrong with any of her systems. That made me suspicious of the explosion. What if someone had done something to my rocket horse? The idea of sabotage sent chills running down my spine. Everyone on the station knew that I was searching for Tayla--or any mention of what had happened to her--and yet they all seemed to think I had something to do with her disappearance. Was it just possible that I had been getting too close to some answers?

I must have traveled 2km or so, the far horizon seemingly no closer than it had been, when my suit alarm went off, indicating that I was almost out of air. I came to a soft bouncing halt, extracted the old canister and inserted the new. I was getting tired. The pounding in my head had not ceased, I was still dizzy, and the effort to breathe--even with the new oxygen--was getting more and more strained as my injured chest muscles heaved with the effort of movement. A brief glance at the edge of the gravel plains told me that I was no closer to salvation than I had been when I'd first begun my journey. I took a deep breath, determined to reach Dover, when my suit alarm went off again!

A frantic glance at my readouts told me I was once more low on air! How could that be possible, when I'd just started a new canister? A chill feeling of dread washed over my suddenly perspiring body. Had someone made sure that, should I survive the explosion, I wouldn't get very far?

I gulped in a dry mouth, considering my options. It was either continue on, until I ran out of air, or take a seat on the rough pink ground and wait for the inevitable. I swallowed again, hefted my load, and turned my beam to the distance once again.

My bouncing progress hadn't gotten me much farther, when my breath began to rasp in my throat, and I knew I didn't have much air left. With sad admission, I slowed to a bobbing halt. This was it.

I dropped the mesh bag to the ground, defeated, and stood looking into the distance, my lantern a forlorn signal of lost hope. I was just about to turn off the beam, when I thought I saw a light wink into existence on the curve of horizon. Could it be the lights of Dover? I waved my beam in excitement, but at a cost. My heaving lungs finally gave up, and with a strangled gasp, I collapsed onto Rareterra Five's pink soil.

***

I dreamed of our vacation on Mars.

I was standing on the balcony of our suite at the Omni Tharsis hotel, mid-way between Olympus Mons and Ascraeus Mons, with a view of the former right from our bedroom. The stay was costing us mega-credits, but visiting Mars was something we'd both been wanting to do for a long time, and we shared the financial burden equally.

Even 600km away, Olympus Mons was an imposing and spectacular sight, although the image was slightly distorted due to the dyplasite dome covering the hotel and it's surrounding tourist district, and I couldn't get enough of the view.

Behind me in the room, Tayla sprawled on our bed, her disheveled hair spread across the pillows like a snow-white fan, her torso barely covered by the cream-colored satin top sheet, her tanned arms and legs askew with previously spent passion.

She made a little moan, smiled crookedly and said in a husky voice, "Come on back to bed, Soefee. Olympus Mons will still be there when we get up."

I turned, saw that the fingers of one of her hands twisted a lock of silky white hair alluringly, something that she knew always got to me. I loved her long platinum hair, finding it uniquely sensual. Her other hand lifted the sheet in invitation.

I gulped and took an eager step toward the bed, but was halted in surprised shock. From somewhere behind me, a cold stiff breeze suddenly pushed past, brushing my bare arms and sending chills down my spine.

Wait, I thought, *there shouldn't* be *any breeze--! This isn't how our vacation went!*

30

Eyes widening in sudden horror, I spun back to the balcony and my gaze swept the surface of the dyplasite dome beyond, looking for the source of the airflow. My questing eyes lit upon a growing crack in the clear protective cover.

But dyplasite shouldn't crack like that, and I knew it. It shouldn't crack at all!

"Tayla!" I shouted, rushing back into the room. "We've got to get--"

But the breeze swiftly became a freezing gale that took my breath away. The dome above the hotel shattered, shards flying, and the gale became a zephyr of wind so harsh and cold that it stung almost as much as the sharp shards. I struggled to reach Tayla, trying to breathe, my chest heaving with effort--

--and started awake, still gasping for air. Ice-cold oxygen filled a mask that was being held firmly over the lower half of my face. I struggled to push the mask away, its presence making me feel oddly claustrophobic.

"Easy," said a calm voice. "Just relax and breathe. You nearly suffocated back there."

Back where? Until that very instant, I really hadn't considered where I might now be, or where I had been. I looked around. We were in a large airlock of some kind. Me and--

The bartender! There was no mistaking that bald head and clear green eyes. It was the bartender from the *Smuggler's Den.*

He said, "My name's Jicob Elfrendini--"

"I know," I managed to croak out, my words nearly swallowed by the oxygen mask.

"--You know?" he repeated, aghast. "How?"

I made a weak motion with my hand. "Name tag. At the bar."

Jicob grinned down at me. "Then you have me at a disadvantage. Other than the fact that you came in looking for that woman the other day, I have no idea who you are." He adjusted something on the air cylinder. "You should be ok in a few moments, Ms.--?" He waited for a name.

"--Sparrow," I supplied, rather reluctantly. I didn't exactly want anyone to know that I'd survived the explosion, until I knew for sure that it hadn't been a case of attempted murder. "Soefee Sparrow."

"Well, Soefee Sparrow," he said with another grin, deepening his dimples, "You seem to have a concussion, you're a little out of it. What were you doing, falling out of the sky?"

"Um a rocket-horse jockey--" I winced.

"Ah. That explains it," Jicob replied with exaggerated seriousness. "Rocket-horse jockeys fall out of the sky all the time."

I might have laughed, except that I knew it would hurt. My head was still pounding, and I continued to feel nauseous. I glanced briefly around the airlock. I was lying on the back seat of an expensive tracked land rover which had been pulled into the airlock alongside a number of other rovers. "Where--?"

Jicob Elfrendini obliged me. "Well, that takes a little explaining. We're in Dover settlement, in the admin sector. This airlock is the garage of the condo where I live."

Something about that didn't make sense. What was a bartender doing, living in the administration section of Dover? Even in my semi-muddled state, that didn't make any sense. And there was something else, too.

"How--how did you find me?" A simple enough question.

Jicob busied himself with slowing the oxygen cylinder's feed, taking his time in answering. At long last he said, "Ask me again when you're feeling better. Right now, just concentrate on breathing and staying awake. Concussions are dangerous, you know." He gave me a full-on blast of his gold-flecked green eyes, that made me feel all shaky inside, and I wasn't sure if it was due entirely to the concussion, which confused me further.

"I don't have time for this," I began weakly, pulling the oxygen mask off, and moving to get up. Big mistake. The action sent waves of pain coursing through my body, and my breath caught. I fell back onto the rover's seat with a stifled groan.

Jicob was instantly by my side. "Where do you think you're going? You're probably not stable enough to be up!" He paused. "You're really pale, Soefee. You could be more busted up than it appears. Maybe I should get you to the clinic--."

"--No!" I exploded, as shear panic threatened to overwhelm me. I couldn't go to the medical facility. I couldn't let anyone on RTF or the station find out that I was still alive. Not until after I found out what had happened to Ol' Betty.

The bartender shook his head stubbornly. "I really think you should be examined by a doctor--."

He was right, and I knew it, but I said, "Look, I only need a place to rest. Just for a few days. I can't let anyone from the Company know I'm still alive. Not yet."

Jicob gave me a piercing look. For a moment I thought that he was going to insist on a trip to the clinic after all, but his eyes softened. "Come on," he said with a sigh. "Let me help you into the house."

FIVE

I must have passed out again, because the next thing I knew, I was on my back, looking up at an unfamiliar ceiling. My gaze traveled around the rest of the confines of what appeared to be a living area.

Jicob Elfrendini's home wasn't exactly what I would have expected of a twenty-something-bartender's place. To tell the truth, I'm not sure what I would have anticipated, but it wasn't this sleek, modern, high-end residence, with faux leather furniture, clear dyplasite tables and a goat-horn chandelier. Sure, I knew bartenders made good credits, but not enough to afford this kind of a living.

"*Bartender*, eh?" I asked, pointedly.

Jicob answered from over by an open kitchen area, and spoke cautiously. "--Part time, yes."

"What do you do with the rest of your time?" He was handsome enough to be a male model, and his refined accent suggested an education far beyond tending bar in a cave somewhere in the asteroid belt.

He came over to the couch on which I was reclining, and his eyes darted uneasily away from me. Instead of replying, he offered me a glass of water and some pain pills, and changed the subject. "Soefee, you've passed out twice. Give me one good reason why I shouldn't take you to the clinic."

I studied his profile, and made a decision. "Because I think someone was trying to kill me."

Jicob almost dropped the glass that was still in his hand. "Wh--what?"

"My perfectly good rocket-horse exploded beneath me today."

"Well, that doesn't mean--"

"--and my brand new extra air canister was already depleted, when I went to use it." I refused the pills, but took the water he was still holding, and sipped at it in the sudden silence, watching him.

Jicob bit his lower lip, frowning, and began to pace the room. He rubbed the back of his neck, then dropped his hand to his side, and turned to me with a deep sigh of resignation.

"You asked me what I do with the rest of my time, when I'm not tending bar in the *Smuggler's Den*." He came over to sit on the dyplasite table in front of the sofa, and gave me a long, serious look. "Soefee, I work undercover for IBCP."

IBCP! I echoed inwardly. *He's an agent for the Intersystem Bureau of Commodities Protection?* IBCP was a division of Law Enforcement employed by the company's insurance provider to ensure against theft of ore containing valuable gems. That meant Jicob was on Rareterra Five to investigate and protect against product shrinkage. Everyone who worked for the company knew there were IBCP agents employed for such purposes, but they worked undercover, and no one ever actually knew who they were.

I sat there, stunned speechless. Just what, exactly, did Jicob Elfrendini know about recent events? I decided on my usual directness.

"If--if you work for IBCP, do you have any idea what happened to Tayla Block?" And I held my breath, thinking inwardly about the mylar note that had mentioned an 'important discovery'. Given Tayla's line of work, that discovery would have to be something geological, something which could possibly fall into the sphere of Jicob's duties for IBCP.

Jicob looked down at his hands, then back up at me. "I didn't even know her name, until just recently, when I'd heard some idle bar-gossip about her disappearance. Then you came around asking questions, and my suspicions grew. When I began looking into it, I found out that the big-wig I'd occasionally seen her with is one of the company's CEOs."

I let my breath out slowly. So. Tayla had been seeing a CEO? That would certainly explain the gift cookies with the red foil wrapping. There was no doubt that a company exec could afford to buy presents imported from the outer quadrant. I suddenly felt sick.

"Which CEO?" I asked in a tiny voice. I was almost afraid of the answer, because I knew that, whoever it was, I was going to go after them myself and, if there was even the slightest iota of a chance that they had anything to do with Tayla's vanishing, I was going to make them very sorry. Very *very* sorry.

But Jicob was frowning. He said, "You know I can't tell you that, Soefee. Besides, it could have nothing at all to do with what's happened to your friend Tayla--."

"--Or everything!" I exclaimed passionately, ignoring his erroneous presumption that Tayla and I were just 'friends'.

Jicob stood, ending our conversation. "You'd better get some rest." He crossed the room, and opened a cabinet at the bottom of a stainless metal shelving unit, drew out a blanket, came back and placed it over me. "I've got to get over to the *Smuggler's Den* for my shift. We'll talk some more tomorrow." He put a com button on the dyplasite table. "In case you need to reach me," he intoned pointedly, then doused the lights and left his condo without looking back.

Settled on the faux leather couch, alone in the strange condo, my thoughts were in chaos. Who was the mysterious CEO that Tayla had been seen with, and did they have anything to do with her important discovery? Was the mylar note I'd found on Ol' Betty really even from Tayla? Who else knew about Tayla's secret discovery? Anyone? Had I been getting too close to finding out? It seemed that, the more I searched for answers, the more they eluded me.

As I lay pondering such questions in the darkness of my unfamiliar surroundings, the day's events began to catch up with me, and I found that my body was beginning to quake. My teeth chattered with the shock of recent events, and I huddled--shivering-- under the blanket Jicob had put over my aching form. Its fleece was soft and warm, an unexpected comfort, and despite the circumstances, I began to drift into numb nothingness.

***

"Soefee, wake up!"

It was Jicob, having returned from his shift at the *Smuggler's Den*, his voice urgent. He'd entered the condo and then, after shutting and locking the door quickly behind him, he rushed over to where I was groggily trying to shake myself out of some nasty dreams.

A question formed on my lips, and I began in a muzzy voice, "--Wha--?"

Instead of replying, Jicob turned on the view screen of his vid-scope, shushing my query, then proceeded to join me on the couch facing the appliance, careful of my recent injuries.

"Just listen!" He turned up the volume, drowning out my puzzled questions, as a news woman, already in the middle of giving a report, spoke in a professional tone.

". . . earlier, a fatal accident occurred today, in the geomining section of the asteroid belt, when a rocket-horse being piloted by one of the Company's rocket jockeys unexpectedly exploded, killing the rider. There is no information regarding the cause of the accident, but the ten-million-credits rocket-horse was completely destroyed. The jockey--Soefee Sparrow of mining station ALT 556--was apparently killed either during the explosion, or when she and her saddle's emergency ejection mechanism impacted on RTF. Local authorities tell us that, while shredded debris from the rocket-horse is still orbiting and raining down onto Rareterra Five, no survivor has been found, and the rider is presumed dead."

I gave Jicob a small smile of triumph at this news. If everyone on the station thought that I was dead, I could proceed with my investigation without any more legal or corporate impediments.

He pointed a remote at the vid-scope, ready to switch the set off, but paused as the anchorwoman continued.

"In other news: The body of a woman was found today, in a mine shaft on RTF, when tunnel maintenance personnel were preparing to close the shaft to further refuse from the mining stations." I inhaled sharply, and Jicob laid the remote back down on the table. We both returned our full attention to the broadcast, as the reporter went on. "The woman's identity has not been confirmed, but it is strongly believed that the body belongs to that of Rareterra Five's leading geologist, 34-stan'ars-old Tayla Block. Ms. Block has been missing for several days, and an investigation into her disappearance has been ongoing. Anyone with any information regarding her recent disappearance or possible death should contact the authorities immediately. Now for a word from--"

I never heard the rest. I sat, stunned and silent, staring at the reporter's mouth, focused on those glossy red lips as they moved in speech, but not hearing any of the other things that she was saying. I couldn't breathe. I couldn't think.

Tayla was dead.

My heart pounded in awful acknowledgment of the newly revealed facts.

She was no longer considered missing, but dead.

***

I could feel my features twisting with the inner agony of heartbreaking grief. Jicob threw an arm around my shoulders, gently pulling me against him, and I crumpled into his embrace, letting loose by crying my heart out on the front of his shirt.

"I'm so sorry, Soefee," he murmured over and over, while I broke down, sobbing, not yet able to fully comprehend what might have happened, or the enormity of my loss.

"No, no, NO!" I pounded Jicob's shoulder with my fist, and he let me, knowing it was only an emotional release.

When at last I had cried myself out, I pulled away from Jicob, and took the tissue he was holding out to me. I wiped my eyes, blew my nose and squared my shoulders.

"I'm going to find out who did this," I swore in an impassioned voice. "And they're going to pay."

"Soefee," he said softly, "Everyone thinks you're dead. How do you think you're going to--"

My fierce expression stopped him in mid-sentence. "I don't know, Jicob. But I'm going to avenge Tayla, I promise you that. And, if you won't help me, I'll find someone who will."

"You're in no condition to--" He began to protest but, again, my look halted him. He kept silent for a long time before he finally continued. "OK," he said, nodding. "I'll help you. I've got connections. But--" His eyebrows raised, his gold-flecked green eyes drilled into mine. "--not until you're fully recovered. I mean it. You might have broken bones. Your whole side is swollen and bruised from the fall--"

My eyes must have gone wide, realizing what his words meant, because his face suddenly flushed a dark red.

"Yes, I looked." he admitted. "I was worried. With your concussion, I figured you probably had other injuries as well, and you do. Maybe even internal damage. Soefee, I still think you need medical attention--"

"--I told you, *no*," I settled back cautiously onto the couch pillows, pulling the blanket over myself once more as I went. So. Jicob had taken advantage of my unconsciousness. I wasn't sure whether to be angry or not, but I knew there were more important things to worry about, than him taking a surreptitious peek. I said, "The explosion wasn't an accident, and you know it. I was getting close to something, Jicob. Too close. I don't have time for medics; I need to keep going with this."

Jicob got up and began to pace about his living room. After some time, he turned to me and said in his refined accent, "Everyone on the station thinks you're dead. How do you propose to get any information, when you can't even show your face? Especially if someone's after you."

I sniffed, then heaved a painful sigh. "I don't know. You're the undercover man; you tell me."

Jicob came back to sit on the dyplasite coffee table, took my hand, and stared into my eyes. His mouth lifted on one side, deepening his dimple, and he said, "Don't worry, Soefee. Like I said before, I've got connections. We'll figure this out together, once you're back on your feet.

Give me a little time to think about it, and to come up with
some kind of a plan."

SIX

They'd left Tayla dead in a mine shaft! *A mine shaft!* I just couldn't get that thought out of my head. For the past ten days, that's all I could think about, as I'd kept out of sight, trying to recover in the confines of Jicob Elfrendini's posh condo on RTF.

The settlement of Dover was small, and Jicob had advised me not to allow myself to be seen, at least not until the news of my 'death' could blow over, and my photo had ceased being shown on all the vid-scopes. His suggestion made sense. There had been a touching memorial held by the Company, aired on the local stations, my work photo plastered on every vid-scope in town. This morning there had been no mention of my 'accident' or my 'death', so I guessed that perhaps all the hub-bub was finally over, and that I was again free to resume my search for whomever was responsible for Tayla's murder.

Because 'murder' it was. She certainly hadn't thrown her own body into that effing tunnel! News reports on the vid-scope had revealed little information, presumably because the investigation was still open, although they did claim that Gai Hao, chief investigator in charge of the ongoing case, was still following up on some leads. I thought that was a bit ironic, considering that he'd pretty much dismissed me, when I'd asked for his help in finding Tayla, and had all but insisted that no crime had even taken place. My fingers curled into fists of anger every time I thought about it, and I couldn't wait to begin searching for her killers myself.

In the meantime, I had begun to heal, the huge black-and-blue bruises on my chest, ribs and mid-section--where the rocket-horse's saddle straps had dug into my body-- were slowly beginning to fade into a yellowish-green. I'd been up and about for a day or two, gingerly going about the few tasks I was able to perform, thinking they might earn me my keep.

Jicob was due home from the *Smuggler's Den* soon, and I was attempting to prepare a meal, hoping to reassure him that I was worth the risk he was taking, in sheltering me. The kitchen area of his condo was small and tidy and very well-organized, and I was reaching into a drawer for a pair of scissors with which to open a packet of mixed spices, when something in the cabinet caught my eye, stopping me cold.

An opened package of red foil gift wrap.

I slammed the drawer, the breath catching in my throat, and squeezed my eyes tightly shut, as though that could erase what I'd just seen. My mind was reeling, my thoughts in an uproar. I stood that way for several seconds, unable to move, as if even the minutest of actions would break my fragile mental stability.

Just then I heard a muted click, and the door to Jicob's condo opened, and I spun around to see that he was framed in the entry.

"Hey," he said casually. "You're up! That smells great!"

I hastily pasted a semblance of a smile onto my face. "Y-yeah. Thought I'd make us some h-hodge-podge."

Jicob grinned, coming further into the living area. "Some *what*?"

"Hodge-podge. Some--something Tayla used to make. Lots of spices." I turned back to the counter, my hands shaking, and tried to pry the spice packet open with trembling fingers.

"Here," said Jicob. "Let me." He took a multi-tool from his pocket and cut open the pouch with one of the blades, then handed the packet back to me.

I took it, trying not to look him in the face, hiding my roiling emotions, attempting to breathe normally. What did that open package of gift wrap *mean*?

"I'm going in to change," Jicob said, then halted mid-way to his room. "You OK, Soefee? You seem a little frazzled."

"Yeah, I'm good." I returned, with as firm a voice as I could muster. "Just thinking about how Tayla used to make this all the time--" I almost choked on the words.

"Ah." he said, accepting my explanation. "Well, I'll be out in a few." And he disappeared into his bedroom to change his clothes.

I collapsed against the counter, blowing out my in-held breath. Who *was* this man? Why had I been feeling that I could trust him? What was he doing with the red foil wrapping paper? I was certain that it was the same shade and style as the wrap that had been on the cookies in Tayla's quarters on the station. Could it have been Jicob who was secretly seeing her? Was he involved in her murder? What was I supposed to *think*?

My gut feelings urged me to get out of there immediately, while Jicob was busy in his room. But where would I go? I was supposed to be dead. How would I explain my sudden presence? Without my job how could I sustain myself? And leaving the condo would mean not finding out how Jicob was connected to the red foil wrap and--possibly--to Tayla. I had to find out what, if anything, he had to do with her murder--!

At that moment, Jicob re-emerged from the other room, wearing casual clothes and a pair of slippers. He said, "You sure you're OK? You're a bit pale."

"Yeah, I-I'm fine. Just let me get this mixed up and put in the pot with everything else." My trembling hands made it harder for me to hold onto the wooden spoon and bowl, but mixing the ingredients gave me the perfect reason not to look in his direction, and I focused my attention on the task.

Jicob sat down on the sofa with a deep sigh of after-work weariness. He picked up the remote and, settling into the cushions, switched on the vid-scope, looking for something to watch. He surfed the g-frequencies, settled on an ambient music station for background noise, then dropped the remote back onto the dyplasite coffee table, and addressed me.

"Soefee," he began, looking to my position at the kitchen counter, waiting for me to acknowledge him.

I just couldn't look at him. My chaotic thoughts were still focused on the fact that I had found what could be an important clue to Tayla's disappearance, and I didn't want them to lite onto anything that this man might have to say to me.

Jicob tried again. "Soef--"

This time our gazes met; his eyes questioning, and mine lit with inner fire. "*What*?"

He ignored my sharpness. "I think I might have an idea how you can continue looking into your friend's dis--"

"My friend?" I exploded, my emotions suddenly boiling over. "My *friend*?" Jicob just didn't get it. "I told you before, Tayla was my lover, not--not--"

"Ok, Ok," Jicob held up both hands, palms out. "The two of you were close--"

"Don't patronize me, Jicob," I growled dangerously. How dare this complete stranger belittle my relationship with Tayla? Tayla had been my--my--

My Everything. That was it. She'd been everything to me. And now she was gone, and who was responsible? This phony effing bartender?

"Look," I said, dropping the wooden spoon into the bowl. "I'll go. It probably wasn't such a good idea for me to stay here--"

"No," Jicob stood up, and came towards me. "It's my fault. I'm sorry. I didn't mean--"

"--Don't." I wiped my hands on a towel, threw the towel onto the counter, and headed for the door.

"*You can't go*," he insisted firmly and, when I turned at the door, he went on. "You're supposed to be dead. Besides, it was all over the news today, that *you* are now officially the prime suspect in Tayla's murder!"

***

"*Me*?" I squeaked out the word, my voice an octave higher than usual. It was official: *I* was Hao's main suspect! "But, if the authorities think I'm dead--"

"--Then that makes you their perfect scapegoat." He told me simply. "Think about it, Soefee. If you're dead, they can blame you without having to look elsewhere. If the authorities find you guilty of Tayla's death, they can wrap-up their investigation."

To be perfectly honest, at this point I didn't know what to think or believe. What if Jicob was making all of this up? What if he wasn't?

"Why should I believe anything you say?" I demanded.

"Why should I believe *you*?" he shot back at me, thankfully not reiterating the fact that I was the prime suspect in a murder investigation.

Clearly, we were at a standoff.

I came back into the living area and sat glumly down on the sofa.

Jicob followed and sat next to me. He said, "Look, I know I promised to help you, and I will. But, I've got to tell you something first."

I looked up into his intense green eyes, trying to determine whether or not he was being sincere. Would what he was about to say be the truth? What about that red foil paper in the drawer? "What." I said dully.

"You asked me before, how I found you, when you crash-landed on RTF. . . " He paused, as if what he was about to say next was difficult. "I was following someone, but I saw your chute open and come down, so I detoured to see if I could help."

"Following someone? Who? Why?"

Jicob put his face in his hands and sighed. "It was in regard to my work--my *other* job."

Ah! An IBCP investigation! It was none of my business, but my curiosity was piqued.

"You were following a *smuggler*?"

"I'm not at liberty to discuss--"

"Oh, cut the crap, Jicob! I'm supposed to be dead-- who would I tell?"

At that, Jicob got up and went to the stainless metal shelving unit, opened a locked cabinet door, and withdrew a portable vid-scope He came back, reclaimed his seat, and opened the machine. After a moment or two of fiddling with the keyboard, a photograph appeared on the screen. Jicob turned to me.

"This is the person I was following the day you fell out of the sky," He indicated the picture with a toss of his chin. "Also the CEO that I'd seen several times in the bar with you're fr-- with Tayla Block."

I looked at the screen. The person in the photograph was a handsome young woman, perhaps thirty stan'ars old, with short, dark hair and an aristocratic nose, whose attire was nothing short of elegant, and I was immediately jealous. So. *This* is who Tayla had been seeing?

Jicob went on. "I'd been alerted to some unusual activity in the asteroid field, and had grown suspicious of this woman several twelth-stan'ars before she'd started appearing with Tayla, and so I was already watching her. But, there's more." He paused.

I sensed that what the bartender was about to reveal to me was extremely important, and waited with in-held breath, until he finally spoke once again.

"This woman," he said, "is someone I've been dating."

***

By now the smell of simmering hodge-podge was permeating the entire condo, and my stomach growled loudly in the sudden silence between us, and I exhaled a kind of whistle at his statement.

"It wasn't a regular thing," he continued, ignoring both the sounds coming from my belly and my note of surprise. "And I had no idea she was a CEO. It--wasn't that kind of a relationship."

I didn't know how to respond. Jicob was saying that the person Tayla had been cheating on me with, was someone he'd been seeing. Someone who'd been cheating on *him*, with Tayla.

"Um," I managed. "Wh-who is she?"

"Her name's Shara Bemiller. She's one of the of the Company's managing directors. I thought we were pretty tight, but I guess I was wrong. When I began to hear talk of some kind of discovery on RTF, Shara wouldn't discuss the rumors with me. I got even more curious when I started getting reports of unusual traffic coming in and out of RTF orbit. I suspected that it might have to do with the unnamed discovery, so I started watching the landing pad. Imagine my shock, when I found out that it was Shara's private shuttle that was doing all the coming and going. Then she began showing up everywhere with Tayla Block, which led me to believe that the 'discovery' I'd heard so much about was something geological, and probably extremely valuable. Something worth stealing."

"Right up your alley." I commented dryly, but went on impatiently. "This is all very fascinating, Jicob, but I really don't care if this woman is stealing from the Company. All I want to know is, did she have anything to do with Tayla's disappearance and murder?"

"I don't know," he admitted slowly. "I don't want to believe she did--"

"--but?"

"--But she's the person in charge when there's a new vein discovered; the one to contact when there's a special lab finding. If Tayla came across something of extreme value on RTF and reported it to Shara, if the two of them were mixed up in some kind of plot to steal it, maybe Shara's in danger, too."

I studied Jicob's profile. "What do you intend to do?"

Jicob straightened on the couch. "I started to tell you when I got home, that I think I might have an idea how you can continue looking into Tayla's disappearance, even from here."

"What do you mean?" I asked slowly.

He indicated the mobile vid-scope that he was still holding. "This is an unregistered 'scope. I can set you up with an anonymous user ID. While I'm at the bar, you can search the data base for personal logs, work logs, anything you think might lead to clues about Tayla's disappearance. You won't make your injuries worse by sitting around here doing research, and you can do some of your own investigating without being seen by anyone. Once you're up and getting around better, I have some other ideas, as well."

I just stared at him, my mind in a whirl. He wanted to set me up as a blank? Was that even legal? I said, "Are you authorized to do that?"

Jicob grinned, his dimples curving around his smile. "Don't ask questions, Soef." He got up from his position on the couch, sniffing. "That hodge-podge stuff smells really great. Is it time to eat yet?"

SEVEN

My hands shook as I applied two thin stripes of black eye liner, but the effect wasn't as bad as I'd expected, despite my trembling. I wasn't much for make-up normally, and had little practice using it, so I was afraid the necessary application techniques might be beyond my limited capability. I added a hot-pink lip gloss to my mouth, and studied the results in Jicob Elfrendini's bathroom mirror. Not bad. In fact, with thick, artificial lashes, the long, black saran wig over my short-cropped copper hair, contact lenses making my grey eyes blue, and a pair of huge falsies, I hardly recognized myself. Even my posture had changed.

I had spent much of the last ten days in Jicob's condo, both recuperating and doing research, while also trying unsuccessfully to forget about the red foil gift wrap in the kitchen drawer.

I hadn't found out much about Shara Bemiller. She was, indeed, a Company managing director but, other than that, there wasn't much information on her. Apparently she'd been with the Company for over five stan'ars, during which time she'd made a meteoric rise to the top. She did, however, appear on several recent station surveillance vids, once outside Gai Hao's security office, once going into the Waste Disposal office, and twice near the station's garages. Knowing what Jicob had found out about her jaunts between Station 556 and RTF, those last two appearances made sense. Still, something about Shara Bemiller's wanderings gave me pause. Just what it was that bothered me, I couldn't quite put my finger on.

Jicob had continued to vacillate between his two jobs, and I'd made myself completely at home in his condo, using his unregistered vid-scope in an effort to find out what had happened to Tayla Block. We'd both agreed that what I'd found out about Shara wasn't enough to pin any suspicions on her, nor was it enough to consider her in any danger from whomever had abducted Tayla.

That is, until I'd accidentally come across a docking vid of both Shara and Tayla as they'd returned to the station, presumably from RTF.

The vid was grainy and there were a lot of shadows, but it was unmistakably Shara and Tayla. Together. My heart was in my throat as I'd repeatedly watched the short scene, and then later replayed it for Jicob. The girls came into the garage from the docking bays, laughing and kissing each other with a familiarity that only lovers displayed. I'd wanted to retch, and could only imagine that Jicob was feeling the same way.

He'd gotten up from his position at the dining table, and gone into the hallway, where I could hear him moving things. He'd rummaged around in a hall closet, and had come back out with a tattered overnight bag, which he brought into the dining area, where he had then proceeded to dump its entire contents onto the table. The stuff that fell out was incredible: three wigs, make-up, two packs of contact lenses, some clothes--and a pair of amazingly large falsies.

I'd looked up with a smirk. "You like them *that* big???" At which he'd blushed a dark red. I continued, "I don't even want to know why you have all these things."

This time it was his turn to grin. "Undercover, remember?" I tried to picture the good-looking man before me, dressed in the gear on the table, but failed miserably.

He'd given me a serious look, and said, "Soefee, it's time *you* went undercover."

Now here I sat, in Jicob's bathroom, my face painted, my identity hidden beneath fake hair and boobs, waiting for his return, so that we could put into action his plan to infiltrate the Company's upper echelons.

***

Jicob, in his guise as bartender, knew mostly everyone on RTF, some of whom had connections on the station, and he had gotten me a communications job in the station's Waste Disposal office.

I was extremely nervous. I didn't associate with anyone in that office myself, but one of the other rocket-horse jockeys was friends with an office secretary, and we'd all often hung out together in the *Perihelion Cafe*, and I was afraid that, if I ran into her, she might recognize me.

When I got off the passenger shuttle to report for work early the next morning, the gray, utilitarian walls of ALT 556 seemed to close-in on me. I hadn't been on the station in almost 6 weeks, but nothing had changed. The usual hustle-bustle of personnel starting their shifts met my ears, the familiar smell of recycled air assailed my nostrils, and the warm light of artificial UV lent pale shadows to the scene, but instead of feeling comforted, my guts quaked in tremors of anxiety. Would anyone realize this was me?

As luck would have it, on my first day at the new job, the person who greeted me in the Waste Disposal office was Millie Baxter. She was the same girl who had given me the dreadful news of Tayla's disappearance, and seeing her again almost destroyed my carefully prepared persona. My heart pounded with nervousness, not sure what to expect of the encounter.

She flashed me a smile and held out her hand, her squeaky, high-pitched voice welcoming. "You must be Kahwren." We shook, and she continued. "You're right on time. As you know, we start a little earlier than everyone else, and our shifts run a little longer, but you'll get used to the hours, and we do receive extra compensation. There's a fridge for any drinks or food you might have, but for lunch and breaks we get chits that are good in any of the eating establishments on the station."

I nodded, taking all of this in, and wondering briefly why I'd always considered being an equipment jockey was better than doing office work. We'd never gotten food chits over in the garage! I gulped, while my heart kept racing.

Millie continued. "If you'll come with me, I'll show you to your desk. Mostly you'll be answering incoming messages from RTF, and dealing with the haulers."

"H--haulers?" I'd been given to understand that all waste was removed from the station and carted down to RTF by automated shuttle, like the one on which I'd ridden when I'd gone down to the planetoid searching for Tayla.

"Yes," went on Millie, "Our long-distance haulers. Those are the crews that take the hazardous materials that result from mining out into space for placement in the sun's gravity well, where their orbits eventually decay, and they're destroyed. It's time-consuming, and the crews are usually gone for months at a time. You'll be their connection to the Company."

"Oh!" This was a phase of the Company that I'd never even heard about. Interesting.

So far, Millie hadn't seemed to have recognized me, and my heart rate began to settle down somewhat. I hadn't had to speak much yet, but I knew that sooner or later, I was going to have to converse with people, both on and off the Station, via the com panels. Jicob and I had decided that, my having grown up on a distant colony, it would be best for me to eschew my adopted way of speaking, and revert to my native accent, so no one to whom I would be speaking would recognize me as 'Soefee Sparrow'.

I tested my rusty former accent. "Do the long-distance crews check-in very often?"

Millie's smile widened. "They do. And you, my dear, will be their new life-line. As a matter of fact--"

She didn't get the opportunity to finish her sentence. She was interrupted by the entrance of a tall, handsome young woman, perhaps thirty stan'ars old, with short, black hair and an aquiline nose. Her clothing was elegant.

There was no official uniform for station workers, but the usual attire was a comfortable trend of thermal-wear shirts, baggy sweat pants, and a pair of soft-soled scuffs. This woman, however, wore a cashmere sweater, wool slacks, and honest-to-goodness real leather loafers! At her ears, neck and wrists, gold jewelry sparkled. Her chosen color pallet enhanced her natural complexion, and her lithe figure was close to female perfection. Her aristocratic features--

My breath caught, and my heart began to hammer wildly again when I recognized that beautiful face.

The woman was none other than Shara Bemiller.

Shara's tone was a nauseatingly sweet affectation. She said, "Jimmer Graham notified me of a new employee, so I came down to welcome her to the station."

Why would a company exec lower herself to checking out the new employee, I wondered, and eyed her from beneath my false eyelashes.

As I was studying Shara, she was eyeing me. She gave me a very discerning look that made me uncomfortable, looking me up and down like a piece of meat, ending with my falsies. Her own breasts, whether real or augmented, weren't nearly as large.

She spoke again, "Jicob gave you a good reference. You're a friend of his?"

"Yes," I explained, giving her the story Jicob and I had previously cooked up. "I'm a bartender, too. I thought I'd take a sub job, while waiting to see if he can get me work in the bar."

Shara Bemiller seemed to estimate the validity of my claim. "How long have you known him?"

Not lying, I answered shortly. "Not very long," I grinned my best grin of innocence. "But he seems like a real sweetheart."

"Well, let me give you a piece of advice, concerning Jicob Elfrendini," she said in a dry, knowing voice. "He might look and sound like the real deal, but he doesn't even *own* the *Smuggler's Den.* He's nothing more than an unambitious bartender, not worth your trouble. On the other hand, what would you say, if I offered you a temp job in my office? One that might possibly lead to a more-- permanent--position."

Something more was going on here, than was on the surface. I decided to play it cool. I realized that Bemiller's offer could be my only chance to fulfill Jicob's plan to infiltrate the upper echelons of the Company. And also the only way I was going to find out what had happened between her and Tayla. I pretended to consider her proposal.

In response to Shara's offer, Millie Baxter blurted, "Hey! She's just starting here today! I need the help, here in Waste Disposal! You can't just waltz in here and--"

Shara interrupted her brusquely. "--I'll have Jimmer send someone else over for you."

They were fighting over me like a dog over a bone, making me feel awkward. I almost forgot to use my re-acquired accent when I spoke up.

I heaved a huge sigh of what I hoped sounded like boredom. "Look, I don't care where you place me, just tell me where I'm working today. The two of you can argue over the rest after I'm settled and doing my job."

***

I wound up working--as I'd suspected I might--in Bemiller's office. Her insistence had met with full-on resistance from Millie but, in the end, rank had its privileges, and she'd persevered. She really hadn't even needed an assistant, but suddenly I found myself becoming her personal aid anyway. I made coffee--latte, actually--ran errands, and made calls.

Shara's new department was located in a section of the station that was close to the main generators and, as such, was warmer than most other areas. It was a slickly decorated office, all neutral colors, faux wood and dyplasite, with a huge view port and its own bar. I quaked when I saw that. I'd claimed to be a bartender, but had no real concept of the duties involved. What if Shara requested that I make her--or her clients--some alcoholic beverages?

I need not have worried on that score. Shara had other intentions for my use.

After we had gotten the day started, and I'd become somewhat settled in my new duties, Shara had come into the alcove that served as her reception area, and stood watching as I went about my tasks. Three times during the shift, she repeated this activity, and each time my hcart leaped into my throat, fearing I'd been caught posing as something I wasn't. Finally, at the close of the day, she reentered the reception area, where I was quietly assisting

54

her receptionist, Gessie, in refilling the mylar printer for the next day.

She gave me a long look and said, "Kahwren--can I see you in my office?" Her eye brows were raised in a manner that turned my blood to ice. Could I really have been found out already?

As I followed her into the inner room, my legs shaky, I gulped in a dry throat. Had someone--one of the day's clients perhaps--recognized me, and given me away?

She closed the door behind us, and strode over to her 'lectro desk, where she pushed a button. "Gessie, hold all my calls." She looked up over the desk and smiled. "*Gods*, it's hot in here today, isn't it?"

I gulped again. Oh. Oh my. I just stood there, letting my surprise flood my face in a scarlet blush.

She said, "Don't worry, we won't be interrupted." She came around the desk, right up to stand before me, invading my personal space with a nonchalance that was pure arrogance. She was only slightly taller than I was, but her attitude of entitlement was nearly overwhelming.

She reached over and touched my face, running the back of her hand along the curve of my cheek. She said, softly, "It's alright, Kahwren, just relax."

She was going to play *that* game, was she? Is that how she and Tayla had gotten involved?

"Wr-ren." I said, putting a false touch of fear into my tone and feeding her a nick-name that didn't really exist. If this was how she operated, I knew the score, and could run with the best of them. I'd dealt with people like her before, both female and male. *You're a big girl*, my brain told me, *You can handle yourself!* I promised myself then and there to give this boss-lady a show that would be worthy of an award.

I summoned up a small shiver, and batted my fake eyelashes in a pretense of nerves.

Shara's smile widened. She tilted her head, grabbing my shoulders in mock reassurance. "I don't bite, Wren. It's much too warm in here, maybe you'd like to-- remove your jacket?" She allowed her hands to slide down my arms, just grazing the huge falsies I was wearing, and slipping the translucent jacket down off my body.

My heart drummed in my chest, frightened that she would discover the fake boobs, and be made aware of my disguise, but they were top-notch fakes, and reasonably realistic in textural composition. I drew a breath and said coyly, "I--I--Please don't." If I was reading her correctly, my mock distress would turn her on, but she'd also desist in her harassment --for now.

Shara dropped her hands to her sides. She said, "There. Nothing to be afraid of. I just thought you might be too warm, with all the running around you've done today."

I quickly stooped and retrieved my jacket then pulled it back around my shoulders, feigning dismay, and blushing for all I was worth.

She went back behind her desk, sat, and said, "Now, tell me all about what you thought of your new job. What can I do to improve your desire to remain with us?"

"You--you mean I--can stay? A-after I--I-- wouldn't--" I let my voice trail off.

"Now, now," said Shara Bemiller. "That was just a slight misunderstanding on *your* part. Of course you can stay, Wren. As a matter of fact, I look forward to dealing with you on a daily basis. Perhaps we can--get to know each other better." And the smile she gave me was as predatory as they came.

***

By the end of my first day, I was exhausted. I'd had no idea how difficult it was going to be to keep up the pretense of being Kahwren Newsum. My old accent had reemerged in full strength, and I found it hard not to use it when I contacted Jicob later that evening.

"I was assigned quarters on the station, so it looks like you don't have to put up with me anymore." I told him via vid-scope To my dismay, however, I'd been shocked to learn that the rooms I had been given were Tayla's old quarters. Worse still, her access card was the very one that I'd used for the almost three stan'ars during which we'd shared accommodations. I knew because I had

56

scratched an "S" on the surface of mine, so we could tell our cards apart, and this one bore my mark.

Holding a cup of something from which steam was rising, Jicob said, "How're you holding up?"

I could see the concern in his green eyes, as I suddenly froze. I'd pulled off the translucent floral jacket I'd worn to work, and had thrown it over the colorful pillows on the g-couch, and then stopped in sudden realization. Those pillows had belonged to Tayla. And her crazy striped throws still graced the bed.

I gulped.

"Soefee?"

The malfunctioning light over the sink started to blink sporadically, almost in time to the insane dripping of that leaky kitchen faucet, and I realized that, despite the lack of Tayla's most personal effects, the place was just the same as it'd been, when we'd shared her bed.

Jicob's soft, husky voice broke into my thoughts. "Soef--?"

"--what?" I snapped back to attention.

"Are you ok? What's the matter?"

"It--it's just--these were--I was assigned to--*Tayla's* quarters--"

"Ohmigod," said Jicob on the other end of the connection. He sighed heavily, and wiped a hand across his forehead. "I'm sorry. Look, do you want to come back down here to RTF for the night?"

"N--no. That would arouse suspicion." I swallowed a lump in my throat, and forced my voice to be steady. Looking around the area with a sadness that was hard to overcome, I said slowly, "I didn't get the job you arranged for me."

"Huh? What are you talking about? You just said you were given Tayla's quarters on the station--"

"Yeah, I got *a* job--just not the one you *thought* I'd get. I'm--a personal assistant."

"Seriously? That sounds better than working communications shifts. Will you still be working in the Waste Disposal office?" He took a sip of his beverage, eyeing me over the rim of his mug, then swallowed.

"No. I'm working directly for Shara Bemiller."

"*What?*" Jicob's voice rose at least two octaves, and he almost dropped the steaming cup he was holding.

Giving him a level look from my side of the vid-scope connection, I told him simply, "I'm *in.*"

***

A couple of work shifts later, Shara Bemiller had not ceased in her efforts to seduce me, and I was terrified that, should I allow her to succeed, either the wig or the falsies I'd been wearing daily would certainly give me away. All it would take, would be one wrong move for the fake boobs to be visible, or for the wig to come off.

I had just gotten back to my quarters after my shift of avoiding the boss's advances, and was standing in Tayla's HC, closely appraising my appearance. My normally close-cropped copper hair had grown-in a lot since my last cut--before my rocket horse accident--and, minus the wig, was now a shaggy red mop that framed my face and curled around my ears. I studied my crown of unruly red tresses. They weren't as straight as the black wig, but, if I used some black dye, they could pass as the same hair in a shorter style. I'd bought some dye with this possibility in mind and, standing before the mirror, decided to use it. I was supposed to be dead, and I didn't need anyone finding out that I was still living and breathing, and investigating Tayla's disappearance.

When I left the HC a short time later, towel wrapped around my head, I felt like a new person. I used some of Tayla's old nail polish I found in a drawer--the cleaning personnel hadn't been as thorough as they should have been--and did my nails. It was something I'd rarely ever done. Using her polish felt like I was connecting to Tayla somehow, and was almost comforting. Although she'd been a bit messy in her cleaning habits, Tayla had also been the high-maintenance type. In contrast to me, she'd kept her glossy-white hair perfectly trimmed, her finger- and toe-nails expertly polished, her figure slim and tight. I thought about how she'd felt in bed, on our holiday to Olympus Mons, when we'd both been in the best shape of our lives, and my breath caught in an unexpected sob.

Tayla! I hadn't thought about her lately, not in *this* way, and the force of my emotions threatened to overwhelm me. Staring at my painted nails, my eyes blurred, and I swiped at the tears with the back of my hand, determined to block out useless memories, and get on with my plans for avenging her.

Nail painting completed, I blew a last shaky breath across my fingernails to finish drying them, but my fingers were ice-cold, and goose bumps rose on my arms. As usual, the quarters were too cool. I got up and put on a heavy robe, then plopped down on the g-couch and wriggled between Tayla's multi-colored pillows, trying to get warm. My hair was still damp and, combined with the chill temperature, I couldn't seem to get comfortable. I reached across the space between the g-couch and the bed, grabbed one of the fleece throws, and drew it over myself.

The next thing I knew, my alarm was going off. I'd slept right through the evening, and the entire night as well.

I rose, stiff from sleeping on the g-couch, and took the towel from my now-dry hair, then went into the hygiene chamber. I looked like shit. I heaved a sigh, and began the process of washing and primping, getting ready for another shift of evading my boss, while trying to find some answers to the mystery of what had happened to Tayla.

***

Walking into Shara Bemiller's office for the next shift, I knew I looked better than I had when I'd woken up. I had chosen to wear a sleeveless form-fitting black dress today, one that normally fit, but was now stretched much too tightly across the chest. It had a high neckline which prevented my falsies from being discovered, but was short, allowing my long legs to be viewed without hindrance, and I wore shiny black scuffs to enhance the look. As had become the norm, I'd applied my blue contact lens and the false eyelashes, some eye liner and lip gloss. Together with my short, wavy black hair, the result was that I looked like anyone but Soefee Sparrow.

I strode into the office alcove, and Shara's receptionist, Gessie, gave me a double take. She said, "K-- Kahwren? Wow! You look great with short hair!"

Smiling, I thanked her for the compliment, and after a few more casual words, we set to work.

Near lunchtime, while I was busy at the coffee maker, two men entered Shara's reception area, and I was once more on edge, as Jimmer Graham and Guy Hao asked Gessie specifically for me. I drew in a nervous breath, and turned from what I was doing, hoping my cover hadn't been blown, to address them.

"Good morning. How can I help you?" I asked in my retro accent.

Jimmer gave me a close inspection. "Kahwren Newsum?"

"Yes."

"You--look different than you did, when I interviewed you."

I crossed the reception alcove to where the men were standing, and smiled tightly. "Haircut." I explained with a little scissor-gesture from my hands.

"Oh. Right." Jimmer pulled a vindex out of the pocket of his immaculate blazer. "I have some tax forms for you to sign."

"Tax forms? Seriously? Out here on the *station?* I thought wages here were tax-free."

Jimmer Graham and Guy Hao gave each other a look, and laughed. Still chuckling, Hao's thick, rubbery red lips parted to exhale the heavy stench of garlic. He said, "I'm the station's Chief Security Investigator, Gai Hao. Believe me, Ma'am, there's no such thing as tax-free wages."

"Oh," Backing away from his breath, I spoke with a sigh of affected disappointment. "In that case, give it here, and I'll sign . . ."

I made to take the vindex Graham was holding out to me but, as I pulled the flat, compact instrument from his hand, Jimmer held onto it for just a second too long. Our eyes met. His were an unspoken challenge. I cast my own gaze down, and grabbed the vindex away from him, clearing my throat.

"Where do I sign?"

He moved closer to show me. Too close. "Ok, let's see . . . " He glanced at the vindex, his head almost touching mine.

At that moment, Shara Bemiller came out of her office. She stopped abruptly.

"Jimmer! Guy! I wasn't aware that you two were here. What can I do for you?"

Graham immediately moved away from me, a smile spreading slowly across his face. "Shara. We were on our way to Waste Disposal, and since we were passing, we stopped to get Ms. Newsum's signatures for her tax papers."

Shara's perfect eyebrows went up. "Really? I'm sure you could have sent them to Gessie's vid-scope, and saved yourselves the trouble." She turned to her receptionist. "Gessie, could I see you for a moment?"

The two women disappeared into the inner office.

I handed Graham the vindex, my own eyebrows raised. He said, "Thanks. I'm sure I'll see you around the station."

"Not if I see you first," I muttered under my breath, watching them leave.

As they wandered out of the alcove, I heard Graham say to Hao, "What a bitch that Bemiller woman is."

And Hao returned, "If she wasn't so careful after that big discovery, I'm sure she would have disappeared, too."

***

So. Shara Bemiller, Guy Hao and Jimmer Graham all knew something about the "important discovery" that Tayla had mentioned in her mylar note. The three of them were somehow connected, through the discovery of a thing which was obviously valuable and top secret. Something that Tayla had been involved in as well.

I had gone down to the *Perihelion Cafe,* just to get away from the sexual tension in Shara's office. It was an odd time of day--between lunch and the end of a shift--

61

and the usually busy place was nearly deserted. I chose a booth in the back, and sat alone, drinking a cup of coffee that wasn't nearly as good as what I could have gotten in the office, my mind in a whirl.

That Shara had seen Jimmer Graham's interest in me, was obvious, and I knew that it would have put a strain on her intentions toward me. If Shara Bemiller was already jealous of any attention I was getting from other people, was I in a position to start asking questions of her?

What was the important discovery that was driving Shara, and which had likely gotten Tayla Block killed? It had to be something geological. We were all out here to mine rubies, pink sapphires and copper ore, none of which was anything worth killing or dying over. There had to be something more valuable at stake, a vein of rock that was so precious it was worth killing someone to keep it a secret.

I had to gain Shara's confidence! It was the only way I would have a chance of finding out what was going on. Perhaps I could use Jimmer Graham's pass at me to my own advantage. If Shara felt that her chances with me were threatened, maybe she'd be more likely to take me into her inner circle, just to keep my affections.

At least that was my hope.

***

When I was finally called into Shara's inner office, near the end of the shift, I was surprised only that she had waited so long to summon me, after seeing Jimmer Grahams's interest. I cruised on in, my tight black dress and new hair style proclaiming a whole new me.

"Wren! What have you done to your hair? Where did those *waves* come from?" Shara demanded coyly.

I looked down, feigning modesty. "When my hair's long, it's so heavy, it pulls the waves out of it." I made a fluttery motion with my fingers. "When it's short, you know, it curls up a little." I batted my fake lashes. "I think Mr. Graham liked it."

Shara snorted derisively, but didn't comment on my observation. She came out from behind her desk. Once again, she breached my personal space with a haughtiness that was unequaled. She touched her hand to my hair, feeling the texture between her fingers, and I held my breath, hoping she wouldn't realize that the wig had been saran, and this was human hair. She said, "I never would have guessed that you'd look good in a short cut." She paused. "Well, I like it. It suits you."

Still continuing to stare at the floor, I lightly brushed her hand away from my hair, and said softly, "Thank you."

For a tense, lengthy moment, Shara did nothing, said nothing, and I waited, my eyes still on the floor, wondering if I'd over-played my demure act, and insulted her.

Finally, Shara spoke, her voice hard. "Cut the act!"

My heart almost stopped. Had I been found out, after all? Had she noticed the difference between the wig and my real hair? It was all I could do, not to look up and search her face for confirmation of my fears.

But my boss continued in a scornful voice. "You come waltzing in here like a diva, and then you push my hand away like you don't want my attention? You want me, and you know it! *I* know it!" She grabbed the back of my head, pulling my face toward hers, and planted a harsh, demanding kiss right on my lips. I waited a long breathless moment before I suddenly returned the pressure of her mouth with my own, letting her think that she'd won, and that I was now fully under her spell.

I didn't know how long I would keep up the charade, but for the moment I felt that it would serve my purposes to let Shara think I was her latest conquest. At least for now.

***

Jicob wasn't too happy with my report later that evening.

I could tell by his clothing that he'd just finished his shift at the *Smuggler's Den*, and his voice over the vid-scope sounded tired and rough. Behind him, his condo was unusually messy.

"Soefee, that woman is dangerous!" he exclaimed. "You've put yourself into a very precarious position."

I shrugged and gave him a level gaze. "I'm going to find out what's going on, Jicob, and I'm going to nail that bitch to the wall for whatever she--or her friends--did to Tayla. End of story."

Jicob looked away with a huge sigh. "Are you sure I can't talk you out of this?"

"You're the one who wanted me to go undercover, in the first place!" I accused.

"Yeah, but not under *the* covers!" he countered a bit more loudly than necessary.

I studied his face closely. There was concern written on his smooth features, his green eyes slightly narrowed. Could it be that he actually cared what happened to me? Or was this all just a facade, designed to cover his real concerns about the Company's product shrinkage?

I said, "Look, I've got everything under control. Don't worry about it."

He was about to say something else, but I ended the transmission.

I got up from the g-couch, went over to the stainless steel section of Tayla's quarters, and poured myself a drink of something harder than coffee, thinking. All day long, I'd been trying to come up with a plan which would allow me to gain access to Shara Bemiller's vid-scope. A way in which I could search her personal files for any clue to the "important discovery", or to Tayla's disappearance. After careful consideration, and another two drinks, I thought I might have completely worked out an idea.

I finished my third drink, washed the glass, making sure to tighten the loose handle on the sink and, leaving the malfunctioning light above the stainless counter burning in memory of Tayla, headed for the bed.

Tomorrow, I would put the plan I'd been hatching all day into effect.

***

I woke up naked and flat on my back, staring up at the strange ceiling of a stay-awhile room. I knew it was a stay-awhile because of the mirrored tiles above me, and the soft illumination from a thin shaft of light peeking in from an ensuite. How I had gotten here, or what I was doing here, I had no idea.

The bedding which covered me was a tangled mess. I moved to pull the blanket more fully over my unclothed body, and my head whirled, bringing on a strong feeling of nausea. I choked it down with difficulty, wondering what in the blazes had happened to me.

The last thing I clearly remembered, was going to work with the intention of searching Shara Bemiller's vidscope files.

As I laid there trying to piece together my recent memories, a voice spoke from a dim corner of the room.

"I'm sorry, Wren, but I had to be sure."

It was Shara. What was *she* doing here?

"Shure've what?" I slurred groggily.

"You." Shara Bemiller came out of the shadows to stand by the bed. The semi-darkness revealed that she was wearing a long terry robe--open enough to reveal that she, too, was naked underneath--her short, dark hair mussed. "I couldn't be sure you weren't a psimmer. I had to know."

"Ahhh psimmm--wha--?" My thoughts were still reeling from whatever was making me queasy, and I had no idea what she was talking about. I cast about in my mind for any reason at all, that we'd be naked together in a stay-awhile. Surely, we hadn't--?

But our mutual state of undress suggested that perhaps we had. My pulse quickened as I entertained fears of what may have transpired between us, and the danger it posed.

"Psimmer," she repeated distinctly for my muddled benefit. "Someone who can project an altered image of themselves into another's mind. They're a relatively new security weapon. Law enforcement and security have been using them for less than five stan'ars. Industrial espionage agents for a little longer. Psimmers can change their appearance in another person's mind--like an extrasensory form of cloaking technology. It takes a good deal of money and effort to train them, and so far they've been a very rare tool." She paused, turning away to pace the stay-awhile room. After several moments, she returned to stand over me once more. "Recently a report came down to me that there was a psimmer on the station. I had to be sure it wasn't you."

I looked up at her, realizing what she was getting at, but then a thought occurred to me. "What--would a--psimmer need with a--set of falsies?" I was naked, so it was obvious that she knew about the fake boobs. If I'd been a psimmer, I would have had no need for disguises at all.

Shara smiled tightly. "Precisely."

"Wh--what--happened--to me? Whaddja do to me?" My tongue felt like thick flannel in my mouth, and, although my spinning vision had steadied somewhat, I still had an urge to puke.

Shara glanced up at the mirrored ceiling, and studied our dark reflections for a moment. She heaved a sigh. "Do you remember going to the Smuggler's Den?"

Brief bits and pieces of memory flashed before my eyes like concise little haiku, almost too quickly to grasp:

> a private shuttle
> all the exits
> secure
>
> the taproom
> raw corundum walls
> glittering here and there in the dimness
>
> miners perching atop metal stools
> their backs to us
> as we enter together
>
> Jicob looking up in surprise
> my reflection in the mirror
> behind him
>
> a table in the corner
> seated across from me

Graham and Hao

a weird pink concoction
snatches of drunken conversation
Shara's laughter

slow-motion motions
every dim light becoming
magnified and smeared

sudden comprehension
what is that odd sweetness
in my drink?

What *was* that substance that had been in my drink? I gasped with astonished realization, giving Shara Bemiller a wide-eyed look. She'd drugged me! The bitch had drugged me!

I made an effort to rise from my position on the bed, but couldn't seem to get my limbs working properly, and fell back onto the mattress, the room spinning out of control, and my last coherent thoughts were, *What the hell kind of trouble have I gotten myself into?* And, *Am I going to disappear just like Tayla did?*

***

Ever-so-slowly, yesterday's events began to come back to me in more detail. I was still on the bed in the stay-awhile room, but now I was alone. Shara had gone--I had no idea where--locking the door behind her. I was still unable to get my muscles working, or to properly focus my thoughts, but gradually my memory began to come back.

I'd gone into work as usual yesterday, my attire a bit more casual than it'd been thus far. I'd known that Shara had an important meeting scheduled for later in the day, and I had figured that, if I could gain access to her files while she was gone, I'd be spending a lot of time sitting at her work station in the inner office. My plans for the day, however, had begun to unravel right from the start. No sooner had I gotten into the office, than Gessie--

Shara's receptionist--had called off sick, meaning that I would have to replace her at the front desk.

Shara had appeared a little annoyed at the news. She stomped her foot and disappeared into her office, then contacted me moments later, via her intercom.

"Wren? Cancel all of my appointments for today--except that meeting I have later on. And hold all of my calls, as well!"

I had done as I was asked, and heard nothing further from my boss for the rest of the morning. *Great,* I thought sarcastically, *I'm stuck at the front desk, with nothing to do all day!* That meant time would drag, until Shara left for her meeting, finally giving me the opportunity to search her files. But at least with Gessie out for the day, I wouldn't have to explain myself, when I disappeared into the inner office for the remainder of the afternoon.

Again my plans had been thwarted. Half-way through the work day, Shara had come out into the reception area, and addressed me.

"Wren," she'd said, "Grab your purse. We're going out."

"What?" I'd looked up from the online magazine that I'd been perusing to kill my boredom. "Is it lunch time already?" We normally ate out for the mid-shift meal, rather than risking whatever the cafeteria had to offer.

"No," Shara smirked. "It's too early for lunch, but we're going down to the Station Mall. We're going shopping."

Shopping? Seriously? Was this routine behavior for the upper-echelon execs?

I pushed back my desk chair, and feigned innocence. "Ummm--I'm on the clock--" I told her hesitantly.

"Yes, yes," Shara dismissed my excuse with a wave of her hand. "No one will say anything. You'll be with me."

So, instead of working, we'd gone to the mall, and wasted time ogling new fashions like a couple of teenage girl friends, and had then gone to lunch at the *Perihelion Cafe.*

Afterward, as we'd sat sipping lattes, Shara reminded me that she had to go over to RTF for a meeting. "I'd like you to accompany me." She'd finished, giving me a firm look that had warned me not to object.

Our work shift was nearly over, but I'd nodded in agreement, and the next thing I knew, we were in the garage, climbing aboard her private shuttle for the trip to RTF.

It was almost supper-time before we disembarked on Dover's docking platform on Rareterra Five. We'd had a few drinks on board the shuttle, and so I was floating along beside her, when we were dropped off by a tunnel-cab just outside the entry to the *Smuggler's Den*.

We pushed open the pub doors and went into the dimly lit tavern--and there was Jicob.

He glanced up from behind the bar, and our eyes met and held for a long, breathless second, then he went back to cleaning some glasses, as if we were strangers.

Not noticing our silent acknowledgment of each other, Shara greeted Jicob tersely, the way ex-couples do, gave him our drink order, and pulled me along behind her to a table in a rear corner. Moments later our drinks arrived. As Jicob placed them on the table between Shara and me, once again we exchanged glances. His look was a silent question, mine an even one that said, *It's ok, I know what I'm doing.* Shara insisted on paying for both drinks, and Jicob took her credit chit, then left without looking back.

We'd only been there long enough to finish our first drinks, when we were joined by both Jimmer Graham and Gai Hao. I'd thought it rather odd that Shara's "important meeting" should include those two. I'd assumed it would be something to do with the Company's management, or perhaps a meeting with sales execs. The men had ordered a round of drinks and some food, both of which arrived in short order, and small talk had ensued while we ate.

We had just been finishing dessert, when things finally got down to business. Shara, Hao and Graham conversed in quiet voices. There had been something that was being left unsaid between the three of them, placing me on the outside looking in. They had continued, discussing a topic that I was not privy to and, uninterested, I had begun to feel my thoughts drifting. Another round of drinks arrived. I sipped, finding mine overly sweet, and doubt that I would have finished it, if I hadn't been so bored. As it was, I had just been swallowing the last of the liquor when Graham and Hao rose to leave. Shara stood as well, and I was suddenly aware that it was the end of our evening. I made to get up, but found that my muscles had turned to unresponsive jelly, and that the room was beginning to spin.

Too late, I realized that there had been something in my drink. After Shara had made a point of letting Jicob know that I'd had too much to drink, the men had helped her get me outside, into the commuter tunnel, where I had then passed out.

So. Here I was, locked up in a strange stay-awhile, and waiting for whatever would happen when Shara Bemiller returned.

EIGHT

I must have dozed off again because, when the stay-awhile door's locking mechanism released, the sound woke me.

Shara had returned with breakfast, acting like nothing untoward had happened the previous night. She placed the multi-colored bag she was carrying on a small table, along with her purse, and greeted me brightly.

"Wren! Did you sleep well?" She was now dressed in a long, warm sweater over a pair of leggings tucked into fashionable boots.

"What kind of an effing question is that?" I growled before I could think better of it. 'Wren' was supposed to be meek but, throwing caution to the wind, the Soefee in me continued hotly in Wren's accent, "You *drugged* me!"

The accusation had no effect on Shara. "I told you last night. I had to be sure of you." As if that simple utterance explained her actions. As if it condoned them. She began taking wrapped items out of the bag, and placing them on the table. "Are you feeling any better this morning?"

"Yeah, no thanks to you," I mumbled half under my breath. I had to admit the aromas coming from the food on the table were enticing, and my stomach grumbled loudly. It seemed like I hadn't eaten in weeks, and suddenly I was ravenous.

With a grin, Shara held out a steaming cup. "A peace offering?" she said. "Latte."

I sat up, hugging the blanket to my front. This woman was insane! I had to get out of there! But my first inclination was not the best course of action, and I knew I had to remain there, had to figure out what was happening, and why Shara had felt the need to 'be sure' of me.

I took the proffered cup, eyes down to feign capitulation, and sipped.

Shara said, "There. That's better, isn't it?" She crossed the stay-awhile room, and turned on the vid-scope. "Let's see what's happening in the System." She came back to sit on the edge of the bed, left hand holding her latte, the other running up and down my bare back, as she gave her attention to the vid-screen, and I had to fight not to shudder at her unwanted touch.

Still speaking in my re-acquired accent, and trying to sound as casual as possible, I asked, "Why were Inspector Hao and Mr. Graham meeting with you last night? I mean, I know it's none of my business, but that was all just so weird--"

Shara turned away from the System news to give me a steady look. "No. It's not that strange. We wanted to be sure you weren't the psimmer. You see, we three operate a somewhat--private--enterprise which we'd like you to join."

"M-me?" My heart pounded. Was I finally about to find the answers for which I'd been searching? Did Shara's "private enterprise" have anything to do with Tayla's murder and disappearance?

Shara abruptly stopped running her hand up and down along my back. She leaned in, her right hand braced on the bed behind me, her latte-scented breath gently caressing my cheek, and kissed my lips ever-so-lightly. She pulled back, eying my face, and for a moment seemed uncertain. Then she straightened, and instead of the hoped-for revelation, she said, "I *can* trust you, can't I." It wasn't a question, but a statement.

"Of course," I responded, putting as much weight behind my words as I thought would satisfy her and get her to continue talking.

Instead, she left her position on the bed, went to the table, and brought back two warm paper-wrapped breakfast sandwiches. She handed one to me and opened her own, giving her attention back to the news.

We ate in silence, watching current events play across the vid-screen. A collapsed tunnel on RTF, new docking procedures on the station, a rise in the price of gemstones. She stirred at that one, but said nothing. I wondered when she was going to get around to telling me about this business she wanted me to join, but knew that

I had better be patient. So I munched on the sandwich, which was actually good, and kept quiet.

After a while, Shara turned back to me. She said, "Wren, how much do you know about mining on RTF?"

I shrugged my shoulders, then pulled the blanket modestly back up to my neck. "I told you, I'm here for a job in the *Smuggler's Den*. I heard I could make a lot of credits bartending in the asteroid belt--"

"--yes, yes," Shara interrupted impatiently. "But what if I told you, you could make enough credits to buy your *own* bar?"

"Wh--what?" I studied her with large eyes, and this time I wasn't pretending. This was it. I was certain that she was about to reveal to me the project she shared with Hao and Graham. Nor was I wrong.

Shara moved across the room to where she had just left her purse. She delved into it, and brought out something which she held closely in her palm, then came back to the bed. Standing above me, she opened her hand.

"Do you know what this is?"

I looked down. In the middle of her palm sat a small, irregularly shaped nugget of some brownish-red ore, the likes of which I'd never seen in all my stan'ars of pushing rocks through space. I glanced back up.

"No," I said with a shrug.

"It's *painite*," she told me in an awed whisper.

My pulse quickened. *Painite!* It was only the rarest earth element--worth over 60,000 credits a carat! I gulped. Where had this nugget come from? Was this the "important discovery" Tayla had mentioned in her mylar note? I gulped in a dry throat, trying not to look impressed.

Attempting to sound bored, I said, "Yeah, painite, so?"

"Don't you realize the *value* of this little rock?" demanded Shara querulously. "This small chunk will be almost two carats when cut! There's enough here to buy *two* taverns!" She stared wonderingly at the lumpy item, then curled her fingers around the stone, taking back ownership of it. Turning to me again, she went on, "We've discovered a whole vein of painite, containing enough ore to purchase several *planets*!"

This time I did show my surprise. I said, "Yeah, but won't the *Company* own that vein?"

Shara was silent for a long pregnant moment, while the vid-scope news droned on in the background. At last she said, "The Company doesn't know about it."

"What?" I jumped up and began pacing, bringing the blanket with me, then spun on her. "What do you mean, the Company doesn't know? How can that be? Didn't their geologist discover the painite?" I held my breath, waiting for her answer. My heart was pounding so loudly it momentarily blocked out the sounds of the vid-scope, and I was certain she could hear it drumming.

Shara turned away, tucking the nugget into the pocket of her robe. "Yes," she replied slowly. "Someone named Tayla Block did find the vein . . . "

"Then--then how did *you*--" I gulped several times, waiting, needing her answer.

"--She reported it to me." interrupted Shara simply. "It was a matter of protocol . . ."

"Ah," I said. "Protocol. Then what? You just 'forgot' to let the Company know about it?"

Advancing toward me, Shara's voice suddenly sounded pleading. "You don't know what I've been through, Wren. How hard it was to climb the ladder to get where I am! They pay me less than the other CEOs, just because I'm a woman--!"

"Yeah," I said dryly. "Real tough, huh?"

"Don't judge *me*, you little bitch!" Her voice escalated from begging to anger. "You sound just like that stupid, self-righteous geologist--"

"--Tayla Block," said the newscaster on the vid-scope.

We both froze, turning our attention to the screen, where a young reporter was just giving a newscast. "Autopsy reports originally identified the corpse as the mining station's chief geologist due to the similarity in stature, but new information from the coroner's office refutes such claims. DNA results and an official expert in facial reconstruction have now identified the body as that of miner, Macy Klevyn, missing since the recent Dover waste-tunnel collapse. Authorities are still looking into the disappearance of Ms. Block. In other news--"

My body literally went numb, and I had trouble keeping my feet. I staggered back to the bed, trailing the blanket, not even bothering to hide my shock.

Tayla might still be alive!

***

Play it cool, I told myself silently, getting a grip on my emotions.

Shara eyed me suspiciously. "You knew Tayla Block?"

"D-distantly," I told her, thinking quickly. "We met while we were both on vacation on Mars, and kept in touch by vid-messages. I--I saw the news reports that she'd disappeared--"

Shara smirked. "Well. This discovery just proves that Tayla was the psimmer--or shall I say Macy Klevyn was the psimmer?"

She'd totally lost me. How could this prove anything of the kind? I said, "How so?"

"If Tayla Block really was who she said she was, she'd still be alive, wouldn't she? But, if Macy Klevyn was also posing as someone called Tayla Block, the death of one would surely explain the mysterious disappearances of both."

My mind whirled. Was Shara really stupid enough to believe her own words?

I said brokenly, "Maybe Tayla's still alive--"

"Don't be naive, Wren! If Tayla Block were alive, she'd still be on the station, wouldn't she? And, if Macy Klevyn hadn't been posing as Tayla, she wouldn't have ended up dead in the tunnel. Their disappearances prove she was the psimmer. And Macy Klevyn's death leaves no one outside the four of us knowing about the painite." She paused, as if considering. "So. What do you think? Do you want a piece of the action? I've already discussed, with Graham and Hao, the concept of cutting you in. We all agreed that, if you weren't found to be the psimmer, you'd be a perfect addition to our --enterprise."

My stomach lurched. If I didn't agree to taking part in their little theft ring, I'd wind up like both Tayla and Macy, just because of what I now knew. But there had to be billions of credits involved in this endeavor, and I knew there must be a major cost to being included.

"Wh--what do I have to do, to become part of your group?" I asked reluctantly.

Shara smiled widely. "Oh, it's all very easy, Wren. First, a real boob-job. The fakes looked fine, but we each prefer something more--user friendly. It's the only way they'd agree to cut you in. Just like last night, all you have to do is be friendly to each of us. Very, *very* friendly."

***

I had eventually given Shara Bemiller my reluctant agreement to consider her offer to be included in the painite theft, and had gotten out of the stay-awhile and back to the station as quickly as possible. I'd told Shara that I wasn't feeling well, due to whatever it was she'd put into my drink the previous night, and she'd agreed to send me back on her private shuttle, but Shara had remained on RTF to finalize something she termed "shipping arrangements".

In my shower back on the station, I scrubbed furiously at my body, but it didn't seem to do any good. I couldn't get rid of the dirty feeling I still endured over what had obviously happened in the stay-awhile on RTF. At what definitely *would* happen again, should I accept Shara's proposal. Her offer was black mail at best; a sick bribe at least.

Before leaving RTF, I had pretended interest in her scheme, and had asked her outright how and when the painite would be extracted, and by whom? How many people would know about it? Her answers had been both unexpected and shocking.

She'd tilted her head and said, "Why, Wren, the vein's already been partially mined, and you needn't worry about transportation to the refinery barge. That stupid rocket jockey, Soefee Sparrow--the one who got

76

herself blown up--is the one who took it to the processor barge without even realizing what it was!"

I'd felt sick to my stomach. I was in much deeper than I'd ever suspected! I'd already taken part in their dirty plans without even knowing it, and now Shara wanted to involve me so thoroughly that I'd never be able to extricate myself!

I'd known then that I had to get out of there, before Shara Bemiller could schedule an appointment for me with a plastic surgeon, and so I'd played sick and made a run for it, back to the familiar confines of the station.

Now, as I stepped out of the shower, I wrapped a towel around my quaking body, and tried to get a hold of myself. I'd thought I'd known what I was getting into, when I'd agreed to go under cover in order to investigate Tayla's disappearance, but I was no longer so sure about what I was doing. Dangerous things were happening, things I had never imagined and had no control over, and I was frightened.

I eyed my vid-scope. Would Jicob be back from his shift at the *Smuggler's Den*? I needed to talk to someone. Someone who knew first hand the peril I was in. I reached out and hit 'scramble', then made the connection, hoping no one had actually bugged my device while I was down on RTF.

The screen lit with the familiar scene of Jicob's condo in the background, his handsome face in the fore. He was still dressed in his work clothes, as if he'd just gotten in, and yawned.

"Soefee? D'you know what time it is?"

I glanced at the chrono display on the bottom of my vid-screen. 04:00.

"I'm sorry," I began, desperate to talk. "I just got back from the surface--"

"Yeah," he said dryly, and yawned again. "Soefee the socialite. You drank so much, the other night, you almost passed out."

"That's not fair, Jicob! You know why I went down there--"

He rubbed his eyes, then gave me an interested look. "What'd you find out?"

"Way more than I'd bargained for. It's a theft ring! Tayla must have been killed over an attempt to bilk the Company out of the profits--"

"A theft ring?" Now all traces of exhaustion left his face. This was right up his alley. "What's being stolen? Who's involved?"

I hesitated. "Is your com channel safe?"

He nodded. "I'm on the blank 'scope you used before. What about *your* end?"

"I scrambled the signal, but--but law enforcement is involved in this, and I've been gone long enough for someone to have placed a bug--"

"Ok. Look. How about I come up there? We can meet somewhere and talk in person."

"Won't that look suspicious?"

"Shara knows you were trying to get a job in the *Smuggler's Den*. If anyone asks, just tell them there was an opening, and I wanted to discuss the possibility with you." His gaze went to the bottom of his screen as though he was checking the time again. "Go get ready for work. I can be up to the station by lunch time. Where do you want to meet?"

"*The Perihelion Cafe*," I said automatically. It was the only place I could think of, that was crowded and noisy enough to give us the required privacy for our conversation.

"*The Perihelion Cafe*," he repeated, then abruptly closed off.

***

The morning dragged. Shara had not returned from RTF, and both Gessie and I found ourselves with little work to do in the office. She answered several calls from the surface which I could only assume were from our boss, and made some appointments. It was the last one that turned my blood to ice when I overheard it. It was an appointment with a plastic surgeon on Mars.

Shara was moving quickly.

Just before lunch, Gessie struck up a conversation with me. I could tell that something was piquing her curiosity, and wasn't very surprised when she ventured a question. "Ms. Bemiller asked me to make an appointment for you, with a surgeon on Mars. Are--are you ok?"

I thought quickly, and tried to make light of it. "I'm fine, thanks. It's a minor matter, but I need to take care of it before it becomes a problem, and she referred me to a doctor on Mars. Unfortunately, I might not be here long enough to even use her referral."

"Why? Are you *leaving* us?" She sounded authentically dismayed.

"I'm not sure yet. I might have an offer for employment down on RTF. I've got a meeting at lunch to find out if it's something I want to pursue."

Gessie's face fell in disappointment. "Oh. I thought you liked it here."

"I do," I hurried to reassure her. "But--the job on Rareterra Five might pay more. I have to find out. It's all about the credits--I need to pay for that surgery." That excuse sounded plausible even to me.

"Oh," said Gessie with a note of understanding. "Well, anyway, I'm glad it's nothing too serious."

"Thanks," I responded, grabbing my purse and heading for the hallway. "I'm combining my lunch hour with the interview, so I shouldn't be too long." I glanced back over my shoulder. "Wish me luck," I told her airily, and breezed out of the office like I didn't have a care in the world.

***

The proverbial clock was ticking, my lunch hour shrinking with each tick, and Jicob still hadn't shown up.

The Perihelion Cafe was busier than normal, most of the tables and booths full. The aroma of flavored coffees and baked goods drifted over the crowd, the noise level more pronounced than usual, due to the high volume of customers. I had chosen a place in the rear from which I could watch the entry, and sat with my back to the wall, fingers drumming nervously on the table, and checking the chrono above the exit constantly.

Where was Jicob?

I wondered more than once if anyone had followed me here. Suppose Gai Hao had bugged my com-unit, and had ordered someone to tail me? As far as I was aware, he hadn't seen through my disguise, but I hated to make that assumption. Jimmer Graham was another consideration. He'd been in HR since I'd come to work on the station, stan'ars ago, and should have known me well enough by now to have recognized my voice, despite the assumed accent, yet when we'd met again, he hadn't seemed to see anyone but Kahwren Newsum. Surely my play-acting couldn't be that good!

I was so wrapped up in my thoughts, that I never saw the young woman who approached my booth. She interrupted my frenzied thoughts with her soft, husky voice.

"This place sure is packed--is anyone sitting here?"

I jumped, startled by her sudden appearance.

"--What?" I glanced up. She was tall and slender, with platinum hair, an olive complexion, dimples, and clear amethyst eyes. Her short, tailored dress fit her slim figure perfectly, its deep shade an echo of her eyes. She was so beautiful, that I almost gasped aloud. Instead I stuttered, caught between wanting to ask her to join me, and knowing that Jicob could be along at any moment. Breathlessly, I said, "I--I'm--um-- waiting for someone."

She was holding two steaming cups of latte, which she set on the table--one before my place--and took a seat across from me in the booth without being invited. She leaned back against the seat, and crossed her long legs.

I was about to protest her audacity, when our gazes locked and my breath caught again. There was something familiar about this woman. She reminded me of someone, but I couldn't quite put a finger on why. I frowned, puzzled.

Her rose-glossed lips pulled into a half-grin, deepening the dimple in her right cheek, and she said smoothly, "Don't look so suspicious. You'll draw attention."

My mouth dropped open in stunned disbelief.

The awesomely gorgeous woman before me was Jicob Elfrendini!

NINE

If anyone should have been able to recognize a familiar voice from an unfamiliar face, it should have been me. Still, I sat there in the brightly colored cafe, surrounded by the lunch-time gaiety of co-workers, mouth agape.

Jicob said, "Close your mouth, before you give us away."

I leaned forward over the table and hissed, "*Jicob*?!"

"None other."

"You might have warned me!"

"Undercover, remember?"

The smirk I saw appear on that stunning face was both unmistakable and annoying.

Memory of his tattered overnight bag, stuffed with wigs and make up and various bits of clothing, filled my vision. I shook my head to clear it, and studied his disguise. Not even the accoutrements I'd spied in that bag of artificial adornments could account for the drastic change in his appearance. My mind made an unexpected leap.

Jicob was the psimmer! I suddenly found the suspicions I'd had about him--when I'd first found the red foil gift wrap in his condo--resurfacing. I gulped. Not for the first time, I wondered, *Who* is *this person?*

Carefully, I spoke. "I thought you said I should tell everyone that I was meeting you--meeting *Jicob!*-- to discuss an employment opportunity!"

"You *are* meeting me to discuss a job! Meet 'Ptommi Young'." Another smirk ensued. "She owns the *Smuggler's Den.* At least that's what it says on the deed. No one's ever met her in person--till now." The clear amethyst eyes studied mine. "She also happens to own my condo. And one on Luna's dark side. Oh, and another one in the Omni Tharsis hotel on Mars."

"Your real job must pay very well," I said sarcastically.

"It doesn't suck." The 'Ptommi' character leaned closer. "Let's cut the crap. What have you found out about

Shara? What kind of a heist is she attempting? Is it ore, or cut gems? Who else is involved?”

I sat back, eyeing the exquisite creature before me, unsure if I should trust him with my newly acquired information. I suddenly realized that I'd never actually seen anything identifying him as an IBCP agent, I'd just taken his word for it. My next statement was soft and quietly enunciated. “I want to see your official ID.”

“*What*!?”

“You heard me.” Much as I hated confrontation, I stuck to my guns, starting to rise. “If you don't show me some real proof immediately, I'm leaving.”

“Wait!” Jicob reached into a pocket of the purple dress, rolling his eyes beneath a fringe of false eyelashes, and huffing. “Soe--Kahwren, I can't believe you don't trust me!” He produced a leather-encased metal shield and sent it sliding it across the table.

I grabbed it before it could skid off the surface, and gave it a quick glance, noting the engraved name: Jicob Elfrendini. “Could be anybody,” I said, with a shrug. “Where's your holographic security ID?”

He fished around in the same pocket and then produced that as well.

He must have passed me the wrong ID, because this one was a Company ID, and it was Tayla Block's.

***

I gasped, speechless. What was Jicob--the *psimmer*--doing with Tayla's ID?

Seeing the shocked look on my face, he grabbed the photo ID out of my hand, took a quick look at it, and groaned. “Look, I can explain--” he began, but I was already on my feet.

“Why . . . do you . . . have that?” I demanded, slowly. At his hesitation, I said loudly, “Answer me, Jicob!”

“Shhhhh!” he cautioned, also rising, and grabbed my elbow. “Let's go somewhere else--”

“I'm not going anywhere with you!” I hissed, as he wrapped an arm around my figure, and began to move me along beside him, heading for the exit.

"I can explain--" he repeated, his breath against my cheek, trying to steer my resisting form in his desired direction.

I stomped on his purple patent leather pump, he let go, and I took off zigzagging through the crowded cafe.

***

People rubber-necked as I pushed past them, leaving stunned faces in my wake, but I didn't care. I had to get out of there, away from Jicob--or whomever he was. I dashed out the cafe doors and down the station corridor, turning corners without regard to where I was going, getting myself lost in the maze of hallways that comprised that section of deck. Not far behind, Jicob raced after me, gaining a little with every straight-away. He'd slipped off the pumps, and ran barefoot over the mesh grid of corridor flooring, gaining traction without the encumbering shoes. Afraid to look back, I kept running, only aware of how much he'd closed the gap between us, when I heard his breath behind me. I made an abrupt turn--

--and found myself at the docking garage doors.

Breathless and panicking, I punched the rocket jockey's entry code into the locking mechanism. The double doors began to open and I quickly squeezed between them, but Jicob slid through before they could shut behind me again, and he caught me before I could head for the lockers to suit up and make an escape.

He held me pinned against a wall, out of breath, lungs gasping for air. I stared up at that beautiful face, my heart pounding, my chest heaving.

"What are you doing with Tayla's ID???" I stormed up at him, still insisting on a reply.

"There's a reason, believe me," he said, also gulping air. "I just can't tell you right now."

I studied his remarkably authentic-looking female facade, with the disarrayed platinum hair, sweat-stained dress and smeared lip-gloss.

"Who are you *really*, Jicob? How much of that disguise is wig and make up, and how much of it are you projecting into my brain???"

84

"I can't tell you that, either--it would compromise my identity. I'll tell you everything one day, Soefee, I swear I will. I just can't say anything until after this investigation is over. Now will you please just tell me what you know about Shara's plans?"

I didn't think I wanted to tell him after all, and I remained stubbornly silent.

"What other option do you have?" he demanded after a brief pause.

I averted my gaze to stare downward, still breathing hard and silently considering, undecided. Indeed, what other options did I have? I couldn't take my information to the authorities--Gai Hao, the Chief Security Investigator, was involved!--and I could think of no where else to turn.

***

A short time later, I went back to work. Attempting to smooth my disarrayed clothing and hair, I returned to the office, Jicob's words of explanation still ringing in my ears.

"Shara gave Tayla's ID to me--in order to identify her--when she asked me to kill her."

Jicob and I had left the docking bays behind. Already our fake identities were probably compromised. The garage's security cameras would have picked us up as we'd entered, and neither of us in our guises as Kahwren Newsum or Ptommi Young were supposed to have access clearances to the bays or the vehicles within. Our only hope would be if I could get into Shara's office, try to hack the system, and somehow remove the damning evidence from the security footage.

With that intention, I'd gone back to Shara Bemiller's office, pretending nothing was afoot.

Luckily, Shara had still been on RTF, and Gessie alone had greeted me on my reentry.

"How'd you make out?" she'd asked innocently.

"Wh-what?" My mind was still reeling over the events that had taken place during my lunch hour.

"--With your job interview."

"Oh. Oh!" Catching on, I feigned disappointment. "It doesn't pay what I thought it did. I guess you're stuck with

85

me." I put my purse on the provided ledge. "But I do need to go into Shara's office. The tavern's owner is going to call any minute to ask Shara for a job reference, and I want to pretend to be her. That way, I can make it sound like they won't want me in the bar, and Shara will never know I was looking around for another job."

Gessie grinned. "Well, I'm glad you're going to stay. Go on. I'll put the call through, as soon as it comes in."

Exactly as planned, the receptionist's vid-scope signaled an incoming transmission. Gessie answered, then gave me a conspiratorial nod. I went into Shara's office, and closed the door behind me. I picked up the call.

"I'm here," I told Jicob quietly. "But I won't have much time."

"Ok," he said on the other end. "I'll tell you exactly how to access the security camera files from your location--."

***

Shara returned to the station from RTF just before the end of the shift, barely two hours after I'd hacked the docking-garage security files and deleted the brief footage of 'Ptommi' and me.

She breezed into the office, as if nothing untoward had happened between us, and I yawned at her, trying to keep awake. I hadn't slept since I'd awakened from the drug she'd given me the other night, and today's frantic activity was finally catching up to me. I wished I'd gotten an espresso while I'd waited in the cafe for Jicob.

Thinking of him now, my mind returned to the chat we'd had, once we'd left the docking-garage. I hadn't wanted to pursue a conversation with him at all but, upon his insistence that Shara had asked him to kill Tayla, we'd headed back to her old quarters--now mine--to continue the discussion we'd started in the cafe.

As we'd made our way back through the labyrinth of corridors, I'd reconsidered my suspicions. I'd decided to hear Jicob out. It couldn't hurt, and maybe it would serve to clear up matters in my mind, regarding whether or not I thought he was telling me the truth about everything.

When we'd reached my quarters, however, instead of continuing our conversation, we'd been stopped in dismay. My normally well-organized rooms, were disarrayed and dark, despite the fact that I'd left the malfunctioning light above the kitchen area lit, and a jumbled mess of clothing, pillows and throws greeted us. I'd walked blindly into the chaotic scene, the usually too-cool temperature serving to raise goose bumps on my arms. I'd keyed the lights, and my mouth had dropped open in surprise.

Right behind me, Jicob whistled. "Whoa. Don't touch anything, Soefee. Wait until I determine whether or not this was staged."

"Staged? What do you mean, 'staged'?"

"You know, made to look like a break-in. Maybe this is just some kind of a warning." Jicob had proceeded before me into the mess, a slim morsel of false feminine beauty in the wasteland of my quarters. He'd poked around in what I supposed was a professional manner, then straightened, pulling down the hem of the short purple dress he was wearing.

"This is real, alright. Whoever did this was looking for something. Do you have any idea what they were after? Do you see or sense anything that's missing?"

I'd scanned the area wide-eyed, the shock of the situation hardly registering on my amazed awareness. I was numb, and trying to catch up to what was happening. My wandering gaze fell on the stainless countertop across the room, and all I could focus on was the image in my memory of the cookies with the red foil gift wrap which I'd found on the counter after Tayla's disappearance. "The red foil," I murmured quietly to myself.

"What?" Jicob was standing beside me, a puzzled look in those fake amethyst eyes.

"The gift wrap. I found some in a drawer in the kitchen of your condo."

He frowned. "Yeah. So? What does that have to do with--"

"--Tayla had a box of cookies wrapped in the same foil." I'd informed him slowly.

He'd just told me flat-out that Shara Bemiller had asked him to kill Tayla Block. The same gift wrap was found both in Jicob's condo and in Tayla's quarters on the station. My heart had begun to pound. Had Jicob killed Tayla? Was I standing here alone with an assassin? I gulped.

"I--I--have to--my lunch break--is just about over," I'd spoken, abruptly changing the subject. I could tell by his expression that he'd wanted to say something regarding the red foil gift wrap, but the moment had passed.

Instead, he said, "I'm not going to go back down to RTF tonight. It's my night off, and maybe I'd better stay up here with you on the station. Whoever tossed your quarters might return. Go back to work and see if you can access the security cameras. I'll tell you how to delete our images. Meanwhile, if you think of anything that's missing here, let me know. It could be important."

"Yeah, ok," I'd agreed lamely, and then--after arranging for him to call the office--I'd rushed out of my untidy quarters, and had headed back to work.

***

Shara eyed my slightly disarrayed appearance as she stepped back into the reception area, after having first deposited her travel bag and purse in the inner office.

"What happened to *you*?" she asked, seeming slightly annoyed at my imperfect form.

I ruffled my short, wavy hair with my hand, to spite her. "I'm just tired. I haven't slept." I groused, giving her a look that said it was her fault. "Do you mind if I leave a little early?"

"That depends," she countered in a pointed manner. "Are you still considering what we discussed yesterday?"

"Of course," I snapped, for once allowing 'Kahwren' show her temper. What other choice had Shara left me? It was either go along with her and her fellow thieves--and their unwanted plans for me--or wind up like Tayla.

"Good." Shara smiled, her glistening teeth reminding me of a satisfied predator. She waved me off with a flick of her hand. "Have a pleasant night," she added in a sweetly affected tone, as if I was actually going to be able to enjoy my evening.

I grabbed my purse and left the office, wondering what Gessie might be thinking about the conversation she'd just heard between me and our boss.

***

When I arrived at my quarters, and slid my access card through the slot, the door opened, and I stopped short. The previously trashed area had been thoroughly cleaned and straightened, and Jicob--still disguised as Ptommi--was at the stainless kitchen counter preparing dinner.

I had forgotten all about his plans to remain on the station tonight.

Moving into the living area, my mouth agape, I said, "What have you done? I thought you wanted to 'preserve the scene' or something--"

Ptommi's shoulders rose and fell. "I know how much you hate chaos. Figured you'd feel better if I straightened things up." He indicated the pot on the stove. "I rustled up some of that hodge-podge you're so fond of, too."

That was the final straw. The pungent aroma of Tayla's favorite exotic spices suddenly impacted my senses, and I collapsed onto the g-couch, overwhelmed, and began to cry.

"Soef--?" Jicob's alarmed reaction barely insinuated itself into my misery. He crossed the living area, sank down onto the cushions, and put an arm around me.

For the second time since we'd met, I cried into Jicob's shoulder, only this time it was Ptommi's. He said, "You're seriously in need of some rest. Go take a warm shower. We'll eat when you come out, and then you can go to bed."

I nodded, getting wearily to my feet, and headed into the HC.

***

The steam from my shower still hung over the living area, as I climbed into my bed and pulled the blankets

and throws over myself. I was vaguely aware of Ptommi's--
or Jicob's--comforting presence as he dimmed the
overhead lights in consideration for my need to sleep.

The smell of dinner still permeated the recycled air,
but I didn't have an appetite, and I ignored the familiar
aroma as I snuggled down into the bed, searching for an
escape from the stress of the past few days.

Moments later, I felt the bed give a little, as the soft
warmth of Ptommi Young slid in beside me, to cradle and
spoon my exhausted body. Or maybe it was Jicob. It really
didn't matter which, and I really didn't mind.

***

Something woke me. The repetitive sound of water
drops on stainless.

The dripping of the kitchen faucet seemed
magnified in the semi-darkness, bringing me fully awake,
and I turned to stare at the chrono. 02:34. A couple of
hours before I had to get up for my shift. I rolled over and
found that Ptommi--or Jicob--was gone.

My eyes strained in the dim room and, sitting up, I
found myself to be quite alone. Where had my overnight
guest gone, and why? He'd seemed so insistent on staying
the night, in case of more intruders. Where was he?

I settled back on the bed, pulling the covers over me
again, and thinking. Who had tossed my quarters, and
why? What had they been looking for? The very notion
that someone had violated my privacy gave me the creeps,
and I wished Jicob hadn't left. For the first time since
Tayla's apparent affair, I felt truly vulnerable.

Thought of Tayla's indiscretion reminded me of
Shara Bemiller, and that led to my memory of Shara's
insistence that I undergo breast augmentation surgery. I
frowned into the darkness, angry. How dare she? How
dare that bitch make such a demand of me? It was bad
enough that she wanted to drag me into her illegal
schemes, but to suggest that I alter my body for her
pleasure--? It was beyond insane!

That Shara was insane was obvious. She was both
a sexual predator and an egomaniac, as evidenced by her

90

behavior, and an echo of her words to me, came back to validate my theory:

"That stupid rocket jockey--the one who got herself blown up--brought the painite to the processor, without even knowing it!"

How had Shara known what ore I had hauled? I hadn't noticed what I'd been hauling at the time, mostly because I'd been too upset about Tayla's disappearance to care, but Shara must have been keeping tabs on the ore herself. Was it she who had ordered the destruction of Ol' Betty? Had she been trying to kill me, in case I had realized what my cargo had been? Had she already seen to Tayla's death?

I tossed around on the bed, unable to resume sleep, my thoughts whirling wildly, trying to come up with some answers, but without success. Frustrated, I threw the blankets back and got up, intending to put on some coffee. Alone but jittery, I grabbed my heavy robe and slid it on, then crossed to the small stainless galley, lit only by that one, tiny malfunctioning light bulb. My back to the entry, I began rummaging around in the dimness for my usual mug.

That's when I heard the sound of my door's locking mechanism being released, and someone entered my darkened quarters.

***

I froze, the hairs on the back of my neck standing straight up, almost afraid to turn around. But then I did. The figure of a man stood framed just inside my doorway.

My pulse pounded in my ears, and I could hardly draw a breath. In the man's hand was the dark shape of an energy weapon. I gulped.

He said, "Good. You're already up."

And I recognized the voice of--Jimmer Graham!

Jimmer?--the station's HR manager? One of Shara's bestest buds. Why was he here at oh-two-hundred with a *gun*?

I gulped again and, finding my voice, said, "Where did you get an access card to my quarters?" I demand the information, trying to sound firm.

"Don't be stupid, Wren," he returned with an aggravated sigh. "I have a master key-card. For 'emergencies', of course." He paused, motioning with the energy weapon. "Get dressed. You're coming with me."

***

Jimmer Graham poked and prodded me through the station's corridors in the middle of the night, the dimly-lit hallways devoid of any pedestrians or possible witnesses, the muzzle of his energy weapon pressed against the small of my back.

It was difficult to keep the fear out of my voice, and I said, breathlessly, "Where are we going?"

"Don't worry about it," he said in a rough growl. "You'll find out when we get there."

After several more turns and a ride down one of the lift chutes, I did find out. We rounded a corner, and I suddenly realized where we were. We'd taken an indirect and lonely route to Shara Bemiller's quarters aboard the station.

Even before we'd entered, I could see that Shara's quarters were the standard kind, but that everything had been upgraded, as I would have expected of her, even down to her door. Instead of the usual hatch, she'd had automatic sliding doors installed.

That we'd been expected was obvious. Jimmer used his master key-card to enter unannounced and, as the door slid aside, we found Shara reclining on her g-couch, casually dressed, drink in hand. She glanced up as we passed through her door, a bored expression on her aristocratic features.

She said, "What took you so long?"

Jimmer Graham grinned and rubbed at his chin. "She wasn't dressed."

He'd peeked while I'd changed, of course, the blasted dirt-bag.

Shara rolled her eyes and said to him, "Don't be such an adolescent perv." She diverted her attention to me. "Are you in, or out? I want to know right now."

92

I knew what she was referring to, and could tell by the tone of her voice, that it was imperative that I answer in the affirmative.

"In," I said automatically.

Shara's lips curved into a slow smile. "Good. Then perhaps you can help me with a little--problem." She turned to Jimmer. "Show her."

The HR manager nudged me toward the HC with the end of his weapon, then opened the door. Inside, curled on the floor of the shower and wearing one of my over-sized night shirts, was Ptommi Young. My heart leaped into my throat, but I glanced at Ptommi as if I had no idea who the hell she was, then back at Shara.

"Who's this?" I asked nonchalantly.

"Seriously?" returned Shara with raised eyebrows, suddenly straightening up on the g-couch. "You're telling me you really don't know, Wren?"

"I have no idea," I lied, my pulse pounding. What had they done to Jicob? The right side of Ptommi's face was bruised and bleeding.

A motion from Shara, and Jimmer pushed me roughly into the HC.

"Oops," she said, with a sarcastic smirk. Then she put her drink aside, got up from the g-couch and came to the entrance of the HC. "You see, Wren," she said smoothly, "I'm beginning to doubt your sincerity." She paused, and then said mournfully, "I guess I'll have to cancel your appointment with the plastic surgeon."

Her eyes shifted to Jimmer Graham. "Shut them in, and keep them there, until I can figure out what to do with them." Then she turned away, as her immaculately dressed toady closed the door behind me.

***

As soon as the HC door closed, I bent over Jicob.

"What did they do to you?" I hissed. "Are you ok?"

He stirred, rubbing at his face. "Yeah, I'm good. I just didn't expect it. Bastard cold-cocked me."

"Yeah, not surprised." I said dryly. I'd always suspected Jimmer Graham of being the kind of pretty boy

93

who would only bully those weaker than himself. "What actually happened?"

Ptommi sat up, pulling the borrowed night shirt back down to knee length.

"I had just fallen asleep around ten o'clock when I heard someone trying to break in again, so I went to the door. Luckily I was awake enough to present myself as Ptommi. Turns out it was Hao, pretending to investigate the break in, but I wasn't fooled. I said, 'At this time of night? How do you even know that someone tossed Wren's quarters, anyway? She never reported the break-in to station authorities!' Hao said, 'Who're YOU?' I started to tell him I was your best friend, here to visit you on the station--and that's when he hit me. He must have carried me at least part of the way here, because I came-to in the hallway just before he put me down. I was able to re-project Ptommi's image into his mind before he got a another look at me."

I joined Jicob on the cold floor of the HC. His arms were pimpled with goose bumps, and I thought I might have detected a shiver, but he wasn't complaining. I said, "I wonder what the three of them were doing, breaking into my quarters? It's not like I have anything to do with the painite discovery. I don't even have anything of value."

"I know Tayla had had a hunk of the ore that was never accounted for," said Jicob, "and thought maybe that was what they were after, but I heard one of them say they suspected there was another psimmer on the station, and when they saw me, they figured that's who I was." He paused. "Well, they were right. Now my cover's blown, and--indirectly--so is yours."

"Why would your cover be blown? Don't they just think you're Ptommi Young?"

Jicob sighed patiently. "They scanned me, Soef. Pimmers give off a higher than normal energy when we disguise ourselves. Normally it's undetected, but they've been looking for another psimmer, so Shara has them using TIR technology. It's thermal infrared tech, and it can pick up on emitted energy. The gig is up, they've got me, and if they have me, they have you, too."

I swallowed hard. "What--what do you think they'll do to us?" Thoughts of torture flitted through my mind. I don't know why, just that maybe because I was that scared. They'd probably just kill us outright, to silence us.

Then, suddenly, two different ideas struck me at once. Both of them were related to things Jicob had just mentioned.

I said, "So, when you're unconscious, is your appearance no longer altered in people's minds?"

"Well, duh!" he remarked. "I have to be focused and aware, in order to project my image. If I'm asleep or unconscious, I can't do that." He must have read my features, because he gave me a questioning look. "What?"

Very slowly, I gathered my thoughts. I studied Jicob's damaged "Ptommi" facade. Something about what he'd said moments ago bothered me. Finally, I expressed my doubts.

"H--how would you know if Tayla had a chunk of painite?" If she had hoarded a piece of the expensive ore, even I hadn't known about it, and Jicob had always maintained that he hadn't known Tayla Block personally or otherwise.

Jicob just sat there on the cold tile floor, mouth open, silent. He pushed back a lock of silky platinum hair, his olive complexion paled, and the clear amethyst eyes shifted left.

I waited.

After what seemed like an eternity, he blew out a long, slow breath. He said softly, "Soef, you have to understand--"

He tried again. "I guess you already figured it out--"

But the third time was the charm, as his features wavered and shifted.

"Soefee, please," he said.

And then I was sitting on the cold tile of the HC floor with Tayla Block.

TEN

Jicob was *Tayla*? He had been Tayla all along? Could I trust anything he'd ever told me?

Half of me wanted to throw my arms around Tayla; the other half wanted to throttle Jicob.

"I want to know everything," I said in a low, demanding voice, my lips thin.

And Jicob obliged. He cleared his throat, and began. "When you and Tayla met, you never asked me if I was seeing anyone, or what Tayla did for a living. At least not until after we moved in together. And you never questioned my comings or goings, either. Where did you think I was, on those long weekends, when Tayla said she was working overtime? I went down to RTF, and worked in the *Smuggler's Den*, keeping the Jicob persona for emergencies, in case things went sour up here on the station. Which they eventually did.

"I began to suspect Shara of corporate theft almost immediately. As Tayla, I discovered the painite and reported the vein to Shara, but I also found out through further investigation, that Shara was keeping the discovery to herself, instead of informing the Company. I confronted her, and she warned me to do the same, offering me a 'cut', if I'd keep my mouth shut. Of course I agreed, hoping to buy enough time to obtain more evidence against her.

"Shara found out that there was a psimmer on the station, but she wasn't sure who it was, so when Macie Klevyn, a miner, and Tayla Block disappeared at approximately the same time, Shara figured that Tayla was really one of Macie Klevyn's psimmer disguises.

"I had been using the bartender persona on RTF to continue investigating Shara from a distance. After Macie was found dead, Shara was left thinking that she was finally rid of Tayla--the IBCP psimmer--and by then I had already made my exit, leaving a note for you on your rocket horse.

"I'm sorry I couldn't warn you, Soef. I didn't want you to worry, I swear I didn't, so I left the note saying I was going to RTF."

I listened to all of this with a measure of disbelief. *Jicob* was *Tayla*? I still couldn't wrap my mind around the idea. And there were still a few things that just didn't quite add up.

I said, "What about the cookies?"

"Cookies?" Jicob gave me a blank look. "What cookies?"

"The ones I found in Tayla's quarters--the ones wrapped in the red foil?"

"Oh. I'd given those to Shara as a thank you in return for her getting me the bartending job at the *Smuggler's Den*. Oddly enough, Shara later re-gifted them to Tayla, so I got them back. When I told you I was dating Shara it was true. What I *didn't* tell you, was that I was dating Shara as *Tayla,* in my capacity as an IBCP agent. As Jicob, Shara only knew me as someone she'd recommended for a job on RTF, and who later served her drinks."

That was *it*? The scrap of gift wrap had been nothing more than a red herring? How anti-climatic! The red foil was the clue which had started me on this strange odyssey, searching for Tayla and throwing me into a world of intrigue and industrial espionage.

I felt somehow let down by this realization, and changed tactics.

"But--but you told me you saw Shara and Tayla together in the bar!" I reproached him.

"Yeah, well, I lied. I'm sorry. When you came looking for Tayla, it broke my heart that I couldn't let you in on anything that was going on in my investigation, but I had to throw you off track."

"Then, you've known all along exactly what Shara's been stealing!" I accused hotly, but inside it was *my* heart that was breaking. Both Tayla and Jicob had lied to me.

"No, Soefee. I didn't know for sure if she was smuggling ore or cut stones. I left the station before I could be certain. I--I needed *you* to find that out."

So. I'd been used. By Tayla, by Shara, by Ptommi, and by Jicob.

It was getting awfully hot in the closed-off HC, but I wasn't sure if the air filtration system was malfunctioning, or if rise in temperature was caused by my heated emotions.

I sat sweating in stony silence, trying to figure out what all of this meant--especially to me--and what I was going to do about it.

At long last, I said to Jicob, "Did I ever even matter to you at all?"

"Of course, you did!" he declared fervently. His face melted for a moment, becoming first Jicob, then Tayla, then Ptommi, then Tayla again.

And all at once I knew precisely what I wanted to do.

I stood up, and began to beat on the HC door with the flat of my hand, shouting to the clean-cut HR man on the other side.

"Hey! Hey, Mr. Graham! The psimmer is in here! Do you hear me? It's really the *psimmer*!"

"Wait--Soefee! What are you *doing*?" demanded Jicob frantically, immediately resuming his Ptommie disguise.

The HC door slammed open. Before he could even say a word, I drove the heel of my hand upward into Jimmer Graham's perfect nose, and down he went.

Stunned, Jicob said, "Where did you learn *that*?"

"Never mind," I yelled, pulling him up off the floor by Ptommi's arm. "Let's get outta here!"

We ran.

I had no idea where we were going, and I didn't care, as long as we were putting distance between Shara's quarters, her minions, and us. The dimmed corridors, with their grey metal walls and industrial carpets, all looked the same, so I was taken by surprise when Ptommi's hand suddenly yanked on my upper arm, and Jicob's voice issued from her mouth.

"Quick! In here!"

We made an immediate right and practically fell into Tayla Block's former quarters—*my* quarters.

"What--!?" I demanded, my breath catching in ragged puffs as I threw an uncertain glance Ptommi's way. "This is the first place they'll look for us!"

"Just have to get something!" explained Jicob's voice. He rushed over to the stainless section of the room and, reaching into a top cabinet, he triggered something. All at once a small interior panel dropped open, revealing a dark little compartment.

My mouth dropped open as well. I had been in that cabinet countless times, had cleaned it, had stored items in it, but I had never been aware of that tiny space or its concealing panel.

Ptommi flashed me a quick grin, and then held something out to me. An egg-sized piece of rough, pink ore.

"I told you Tayla had a chunk of painite." Jicob turned away from me, quickly closed the panel, and then shut the cabinet door. "Let me grab some clothes; then we've got to move before they find us!"

"Where are we going?"

"To Shara's Corporate meeting," he said simply, and once again Ptommi's features pulled into an impish smile.

***

By the time we reached the admin section of the station, Jicob was again himself. Gone were Ptommi's long, platinum hair, bare tanned legs, and clear amethyst eyes, replaced by Jicob's gold-flecked green eyes, shaved head and deep dimples. He had changed from the borrowed night shirt Ptommi had been wearing and was now dressed in a forest green jumpsuit that enhanced his physique. As we sauntered into the admin lobby, Jicob's gait was a confident and steady swagger, mine the timid tip-toe of trepidation.

At the smooth, dyplasite electro-desk, Jicob flashed his Corporate ID. There was a brief hesitation as the woman behind the desk gave his identification a quick glance, and then a small gasp escaped her at the gold IBCP badge accompanying the ID. She gave Jicob an astonished look, and then her stunned eyes slid questioningly to me.

Tossing his chin at me, Jicob said, "She's with me." The receptionist nodded, tight-lipped, then pressed a button on her 'lectro desk and we were admitted without further ado.

The Corporate offices aboard Space Mining Station ALT 556 were located at the very top of the central hub, and had a literal "glass ceiling" of dyplasite which displayed a perfect view of Rareterra Five and a few of the smaller asteroids that were currently being mined. From this vantage point one could watch rocket horses zipping about through the vacuum of space, and the refinery barges crushing ore. Inside the CEO's office, and just below the dyplasite dome, the crescent of a polished-ebony desk sat atop a circular carpet emblazoned with the familiar Company logo. Within the black crescent sat the CEO himself and arranged around the semi-circle were a number of comfortable chairs.

I took in the occupants of those seats, and my heart sank. Shara Bemiller, Guy Hao and Jimmer Graham— rubbing his chin—were all present and accounted for. They were circling their proverbial wagons, and had come here to cover their asses.

The door hissed quietly as we entered, not alerting them to our presence and Guy Hao was saying, "—all of my staff are presently searching the station. There're only two of the thieves, and the station's on lockdown, so it shouldn't be any trouble to find them."

Evan Stone, the CEO, was a large man in his middle fifties with shock-white hair and piercing eyes. He was sitting stiffly erect, a displeased look on features that might have been kind under different circumstances. His voice bellowed as he spoke.

"Thieves? On *my* station? The Corporation will have my head! What happened to the IBCP *psimmer* that we employ to prevent shrinkage?"

"I'm right here," spoke Jicob from our position by the door.

Everyone turned, startled. The CEO stood.

"Elfriendini! *You?* You're our undercover man? You —you were listening to all of our private meetings at the bar on RTF?"

Jicob grinned. "None other."

"What are you doing *here*? Why aren't you out there trying to find the thieves that just stole our—" He spluttered to a stop, reseating himself, then began again. "Until only a few moments ago, even *I* hadn't known about the significant discovery on Rareterra Five! And now, they've made away with the—" But he couldn't bring himself to pronounce the magic word, and his booming voice trailed away, confused.

I stood watching Jicob, wondering how he was going to handle this situation. He remained poised, hands in the pockets of his green jumpsuit, a slight smile on his calm features.

Two syllables dropped casually from his lips. "Painite."

Stone's eyes widened, and he gasped aloud. "You *know* about that???"

Jicob moved further into the round office as Shara Bemiller sat looking stunned and more than a bit frightened.

Guy Hao frowned darkly. "Evan! Surely you're not going to listen to this—this—*bartender*!"

"The three fools sitting here are your thieves," informed Jicob evenly.

Shara Bemiller immediately shot to her feet. "He's lying! He has no proof!"

"Here's my proof," said Jicob, and took an egg-sized chunk of pink ore out of his right pocket. "I found this in Tayla Block's quarters."

"—But we *searched* her quarters!" spat Jimmer Graham vehemently, incriminating both himself and the other two.

"Oh, dear God," moaned Shara, sitting back down and covering her eyes with a hand.

Guy Hao jumped in. "Then *Tayla Block* was the thief, as I suspected all along!"

"Tayla Block?" questioned Evan Stone. "Who's Tayla Block?"

"That miserable geologist," said Shara through tight lips. "That bitch! She discovered the painite, but got herself killed. Probably by your precious *psimmer*, Evan."

The CEO's face registered doubt, and his questioning eyes went to Jicob. "Do you have anything to say to these accusations, Elfriendini?"

Jicob tilted his head as he studied Shara Bemiller. "You're gonna stick to your story, then?" He tossed the painite up and down in his right hand, not seeming worried about the charges being leveled at him. His gaze met Stone's. "Ask Ms. Newsum, here, what she knows."

"Newsum?" The CEO gave me a hard look. "Who the *hell* are *you*?" Apparently Evan Stone was so high up in the Corporation he didn't know who any of his employees were.

Shara suddenly smirked. "Kahwren! My dear—" She met my glance with a pleading one of her own. "I gave her a job in my office, Evan. She's—she's one of my favorite employees, aren't you, Wren?" And I could tell by her tone that she felt she still had some kind of hold over me, but I wasn't sure just what it was, and I was determined not to be blackmailed by her again.

I said, "It's Sparrow, actually. Soefee Sparrow. And I'm a rocket-horse jockey."

"S-s-sparrow!" Jimmer Graham stuttered. "But—but, you're *dead*!"

Shara paled, and then a dogged look crossed her elite features. "Sparrow," she said slowly, tasting the name on her tongue, her mind seeming to race behind her façade of aristocratic privilege. Then a triumphant fire leaped into her eyes, as she seemed to add something up in her mind, and I suddenly remembered her telling me that it had been *me* who had unwittingly transported the painite to the refinery barge, making me an automatic accomplice in their plot. "Careful," She warned me in a dangerous hiss.

Jicob and I exchanged glances, and then I made direct eye contact with the CEO.

I blurted out the truth. "I unknowingly moved the painite to one of the barges for them. And my efforts were rewarded with an attempt to murder me. These three blew up my rocket-horse, nearly killing me in the process."

Hao slammed his beefy fist onto the polished ebony desk, his triple chins trembling. "You have no proof of that!"

Evan Stone's eyes never left my face. "*Do* you have any proof?"

I wavered. Did I? Again, I glanced at Jicob.

He said, "The investigation into Soefee Sparrow's "death" was stalled. The proof is in Hao's files." My eyes nearly bugged out of my sockets, and his dimples deepened with his spreading smile as he looked my way. "I guess I didn't tell you *every*thing, Soef." He removed his left hand from his pocket and threw a rec-drive onto Stone's desk. "That's just a copy, by the way."

"This is madness!" shouted Hao, leaping to his feet.

"Siddown," grumbled the CEO, and Hao sat.

Jimmer Graham suddenly spoke. "How do you know this guy's even the psimmer, Evan?"

"Indeed," said, Stone. His eyes traveled up and down the length of Jicob's persona. "As far as I know, you're just a guy who works in a bar."

"Easy," Jicob told them. He placed his ID and badge on Stone's desk for all to see, and his gold-flecked green eyes took on a look of concentration. In mere moments his features changed from those of Jicob Elfriendini to Tayla's to Ptommi's and back again.

Evan Stone stared at Jicob and then at his identifying credentials. He sighed. "Ok, Elfriendini. Give me the whole story."

And Jicob began to outline his mission and what it had entailed, beginning with his discovery—as Tayla Block —of the painite, and ending with our capture by Jimmer Graham.

"You," said Stone harshly to me. "How did *you* get involved in all of this?"

So I told him about Tayla's disappearance, and that small piece of red foil gift wrap which had started me asking questions about her whereabouts, and leading me to my partnership with Jicob Elfriendini.

"All of this has to be reported to the System authorities," said the CEO. "In the meantime," he pressed a button beneath the edge of his ebony desk, "You will all be detained by my personal security team."

"—But!" I began, but Jicob placed a hand on my arm, silencing my protest.

"It'll all be straightened out," he said so softly that only I could hear, and I unhappily desisted, choosing to trust him one more time.

***

Five weeks later, I found myself enjoying a holiday at the Omni Tharsis hotel on Mars. The exact place where Tayla and I had once vacationed, the same condo I now knew to be owned by Ptommi Young.

We had registered at the hotel's front desk as Ptommi Young and Wren Newsum, but had spent the night as Tayla Block and Soefee Sparrow, renewing our former relationship, carefully trying not to repeat any of our previous mistakes. I found that my love for Tayla had grown with her absence, and I was prepared to sacrifice my own OCD ways in return for earning back her love; whatever it took to regain the relationship I had lost. Jicob had always seemed pleased with me, and—after all that we had been through together—I felt that perhaps Tayla could still share those feelings as well.

Earlier in the day, I had asked her why—in all the stan'ars we'd slept together on the station—I'd never woken to find someone else in our bed instead of her. Why hadn't I found one of her other personalities sleeping beside me? Jicob had once told me that, in repose, a psimmer was unable to project a false image, so I suppose I was hoping in my heart to learn that "Tayla" was their core identity. Instead, she'd told me that the more a person saw a certain "aspect" of a psimmer, the more that aspect became ingrained in the person's psyche, and the more likely they were to see only that identity, unless the psimmer consciously projected a different one to them.

Beside me, Tayla Block now lounged, her perfectly tanned body glistening under the dome lights, a stunning view of Olympus Mons as her backdrop. I drank in the sight of her perfect figure and long, platinum hair. If this identity was the one that was now embedded in my subconscious, I could certainly live with that.

But I had also come to realize that, like "Jicob" and "Ptommi", "Tayla" was a false persona. I had to wonder: Exactly who *was* this mysterious IBCP agent??? I gave Tayla—lying on the hotel lenai before the incredible view of Olympus Mons—a long look of consideration. Who was she or he *actually*?

You know what? I found that I didn't really care.

t.santitoro edits the minimalist genre poetry magazine, Scifaikuest. She inhabits a crazy world where horses of a different color exist for real, cats bring surprising gifts to the door, and little grey dogs can change the world. She has a strange fascination with everything Hawaiian, and has a collection of Hawaiian shirts. As an illustrator (aka 7ARS), author and editor, she composes and/or illustrates strange tales about everything from aliens to vampires. She plays ukulele, guitar and bass, uses her computer to enhance her artwork, and sprays stories onto her laptop in the hopes of sharing them with the world. As a poet, she is also known as sakyu.